Philip Gaskell

A Lion Among the Ladies

A Novel: Vol.III.

Philip Gaskell

A Lion Among the Ladies
A Novel: Vol. III.

ISBN/EAN: 9783337066093

Printed in Europe, USA, Canada, Australia, Japan

Cover: Foto ©Andreas Hilbeck / pixelio.de

More available books at **www.hansebooks.com**

A LION AMONG THE LADIES.

A NOVEL.

BY

PHILIP GASKELL,

AUTHOR OF "THE SENIOR MAJOR," ETC.

"A lion among ladies is a most dreadful thing; for there
is not a more fearful wild fowl than your lion living."
Midsummer Night's Dream.

IN THREE VOLUMES.

VOL. III.

LONDON:
F. V. WHITE & CO.,
31 SOUTHAMPTON STREET, STRAND, W.C.

1888.

EDINBURGH

COLSTON AND COMPANY

PRINTERS

CONTENTS.

A LION AMONG THE LADIES.

A LION AMONG THE LADIES.

—o—

CHAPTER I.

SIR WILFRED ASKS A QUESTION.

SIR WILFRED'S first impulse after Guy Leycester's departure was to seek his wife, and once more endeavour to obtain from her some solution of the mystery which in his opinion still shrouded the affair of the diamond robbery. To his annoyance, and

VOL. III.   A somewhat also to his surprise, he found, after his short absence, the drawing-room empty. "Her ladyship had walked out," a footman, on being interrogated, replied; and the Colonel, feeling restless and impatient, proceeded forthwith to imitate her example.

In the near neighbourhood of the barracks, he, having bent his steps in that direction, chanced to fall in with Captain Elphinstone and Guy Leycester. They were apparently engaged in earnest conversation—so earnest indeed that it was not till Sir Wilfred was within a yard of them that they noticed his approach.

"What! back already, Leycester?" exclaimed the Colonel, as the three men stood together near the barrack gate, but out of hearing of the sentry on duty. "I fancied there was metal more attractive at Ivy Cottage than your short visit implies; but perhaps you have come to learn how the interesting patient whom you so nearly sent to kingdom come is going on."

"Confound the fellow!" answered Guy surlily, for Sir Wilfred's chaffing remark regarding May Durant had struck upon a sensitive chord; "he isn't worth thinking about—"

"That's true, poor devil," put in Elphinstone; "but, all the same, that blow on the head was no joke, and if erysipelas (as as one time Braithwaite feared would be the case) *had* set in, you would have been perhaps tried for manslaughter, old man, and most probably convicted too, which, as you must allow, would have been no joke. I dislike the fellow as much as you do, but, for your sake, I wanted to see how he was, as the Yankees say, getting along, and that is the reason why I did not refuse to go when he sent for me."

"By Jove!" exclaimed Sir Wilfred, "I doubt your going, if you had known as much about the man as Leycester and I do. The fact is—only as I don't wish the story to become generally known, I trust to you two fellows to keep it to yourselves—that Brereton is the man who stole the diamonds."

"Not really! By Heavens, what a frightful idea! Why we have been associating with him as if he were a gentleman—"

"Well," interrupted the Colonel, "we are not the first persons who have entertained a robber unawares. Do you re-

member the convict who used to hob
and nob in the Isle of Wight with the
Colonel of Volunteers, and accompany
her ladyship, his wife, upon the fiddle?
We must, to a certain degree, take our
chance in this world as to what class our
intimates may belong; but, Leycester, it
would, I think, be advisable, seeing that
I am due elsewhere, to enlighten Elphinstone on the subject of Major Brereton's
offence. His guilt was not revealed to
me in confidence, and therefore—on the
principle that a *little* knowledge is a
dangerous thing—I recommend to you
this course of proceeding."

"He spoke to me," said Elphinstone,
as the Colonel, with a slight military
salute, moved away, "of applying for
sick leave—"

"Which is, of course, preparatory to

sending in his papers," rejoined Leycester, who then, taking his brother Captain's arm, walked him away to a spot better fitted for confidential intercourse than was the one in which they had been previously discoursing.

It is unnecessary to repeat the conversation which then and there, in reference to Miss Vidal's communication concerning Major Brereton, took place. Of its substance the reader is already aware, and also of the fact (one of which Rowley Elphinstone had been previously ignorant) that Guy's more than suspicion of the Major's guilt had caused the quarrel from the effects of which the latter was still suffering.

"And now, my dear fellow," said Helen Durant's betrothed, and his voice as he uttered the short exordium was lowered, and his manner slightly suggestive of hesitation, " I have something on your, or rather on our, account to say to you : May Durant, whose brother and protector I hope so soon to be—"

" Oh, for God's sake, Rowley," broke in Guy, " do not speak to me of her ! Mrs Durant has more than once told me, in womanly words, but the name does not affect the thing, that I have behaved like a scoundrel. She may not be very far wrong, but you, at least, might find excuses for me. You are a rich man, so that in falling in love you have not behaved like a villain."

" My dear boy, you cannot compare the cases," interrupted Elphinstone. " I can afford the expensive luxury of a wife, and you cannot ; and, therefore, your having engaged the affections of a girl so

young and so ignorant of the world as
is May, cannot, I think, and as even
you must feel, be justified."

"Perhaps not," Guy gloomily responded; "but you reason as if our
hearts and impulses invariably led us to
do the right and proper thing, whereas
my experience tells me that the contrary is the case."

"Granted; but for May's sake, should
you not have endeavoured to conquer
those impulses? You have, for her, poor
child, sown the seeds of much future
sorrow—"

"On the contrary," Guy said doggedly,
"she has been happier since—since I
have known her, than she had ever been
before; but do not let us talk about
her. Rowley. The decree that I am not
to see her again has gone forth, and

the subject is to me, as you may suppose, too painful to be discussed."

"I quite understand that it must be, nor should I have alluded to it but for a request of Mrs Durant's that I would do so."

"Oh! Mrs Durant asked you, did she? to speak to me about her daughter."

"Yes. She wished you to be told that personally she likes you much—"

"It is extremely kind of her to say so," Leycester grimly rejoins.

"Indeed, my dear Guy, you are a favourite with all of us."

"I am awfully grateful to you all."

"And she—Mrs Durant—promises that if May should take to heart your leaving without bidding her good-bye, she shall be informed of the truth—namely, that your doing so was greatly *à contre cœur*, and that you only acted in obedience to her mother's wishes. I assure you that we regret, as much as you can do, that insuperable objections to any engagement on your part with May not only now, but must, I fear, always exist."

"But why, I ask, *must* they always exist? I may—as other men have done —get on."

"And you may—forgive me, my dear boy, for alluding to anything so melancholy, but—"

"I may go off," interpolated Leycester, and the smile which curled his handsome lip was not devoid of bitterness. "You are right there, but I must take my chance with the rest. In the meantime, let me beg of you to say no more to me about this scoundrelly conduct of mine. I have been a fool, and, in your opinion, something worse; but I am having my punishment, and I would much prefer taking it in my own way."

It had been sorely against his will that Rowley Elphinstone had undertaken the commission which Mrs Durant had given him to execute. His own position as a happy and prosperous lover militated—as a man of delicate sensibilities could not fail to understand—against the success of his mission: moreover, the wound was, in poor Guy's case, too recent for even the tenderest hand to probe its depths, without inflicting added suffering. Elphinstone possessed a heart that was almost womanly in its tenderness and power to sympathise with the griefs of others, and being himself very deeply in love, his pity for Guy's sorrows was far greater than he

chose to express in words. There came,
however, a day—and that all too soon—
when he sorely regretted that the last
words which on the subject of Guy's short-
comings he had addressed to his friend
had not been dictated more by the feelings of his heart than by the reasonings
of his head.

.   .   .   .

It was with a slow and lagging step
that Sir Wilfred Gregorie, after leaving
his two interlocutors, proceeded on his
return to his home. Deep in his inner
man there existed, unknown to himself, a
vague and to him totally unaccustomed
sensation of fear. It was so new to him
to feel, even in the very slightest degree,
suspicious of his wife, that, conscious as
he was that his conversation with her
might throw what to him would be an

odious light on a ghastly subject, he for
the first time in his life failed to view
with pleasure (as Florence came forward
in the drawing-room to meet him), the
lovely face of his possibly erring wife.

"Florence," he began, not unkindly,
but the agitated woman felt that the
tones of his voice were strangely stern
and cold, "I have come to question you.
Sit down," he added, as he took a chair
in front of her sofa, "for you are looking pale and worried, which is not surprising, considering the confidence with
which your friend Miss Vidal kindly
honoured us.   Even previous to that
confession on her part of Major Brereton's guilt and of her own, I had seen
and heard much that puzzled me, and
it is to be enlightened on these sub-
jects that I have come to you now.

Had you—before Major Brereton joined
the Regiment — ever spoken to the
man? It is terrible to think that your
name may possibly be, in the very slightest degree mixed up in this atrocious
business; and if such a misfortune should
occur—" but at that moment Lady Gregorie's face, which had hitherto been par-
tially hidden by the large fan she held,
became—through the fall from her hand
of the temporary shield, fully exposed to
view, and the expression of terror that
was plainly written on her countenance
there, went near to rousing the demon
of suspicion in her husband's breast.
Perfectly colourless, save for two crimson
patches which, in ghastly contrast to their
wanness, seemed, as it were, *painted* on
her quivering cheeks, was the face of the
painfully agitated woman. So changed,

indeed, was in a few short moments her appearance, that Sir Wilfred, had it not been for the fiercer passion that, namely, of jealous suspicion which was at work within him, could hardly have viewed the sudden alteration without alarm. As it was, a sensation nearly akin to bewilderment—and one which to his well-balanced nerves was as new as it was strange—crept over him, and this feeling was not decreased when the innocent yet conscience-stricken woman flung herself with a piteous cry at his feet.

Could, he asked himself, his short search be over? And could this cowering creature on whose awful transformation he was gazing be "the woman" whose sin had found her out? It was in answer to this unspoken question that he heard himself exclaim (for the words seemed to break from him without his own volition),—

"Oh, my God! Florence, tell me in mercy that it is not true! I have trusted you so entirely,—have believed in your purity as I have believed in Gospel truth, and to doubt you now will, I think, drive me mad!"

"But you need not doubt me; indeed, *indeed*, you may trust me still," she, enboldened by his softened tone, found courage enough to say. "I have been weak and foolish, but, with the exception of deceiving you— Nay, hear me out, dear; hear me take God to witness that of no act of my life have I reason to feel ashamed. I wish—oh, how I wish, that you could look into my heart, for I feel sure that you would believe me then."

"But you have owned that you deceived me?"

"Yes; because I was silly, and afraid of your displeasure, when, if I had only confided to you the truth—"

"Confide it to me now then," he said sternly, "and make amends, if you can, for the crime and misery which you have caused."

It was under these inauspicious circumstances, and with the austere words which I have just quoted ringing in her ears, that poor Florence related, as best she could, and with perfect truthfulness, the story of her girlish folly.

And Sir Wilfred, although he suffered as only a proud man could under the infliction, was unable, as he looked into her candid eyes, to do other than believe her. He remained perfectly silent during the narration, which Lady Gregorie, in her haste and alarm, cut short, and when it was over, he said, with apparent composure,—

"And the letters? I should like to see them. We shall have paid dearly enough for their possession. I do not allude to the diamond loss—*that* I look upon as nothing—but, as proof to me of your truthfulness, Florence, I hope that you have them in safe keeping."

Now Lady Gregorie, weak as in many respects she had proved herself to be, was not altogether devoid of spirit. Now, too, that the worst was over, some power of self-assertion returned to her. Sir Wilfred's demand for proofs of her innocence angered her, and drawing up her small head proudly, she said, not without some trepidation, and a considerable amount of remorse for her impulsive folly,—

"I am very sorry. I wish you *could* see them, but—and oh, do not be angry Wilfred!—I was so ashamed of them, and so glad to get them back, that I threw the hateful things into the fire. If you wish to know what were the idiotic words I wrote, you can ask Emily Vidal—for she saw me write them—whether all I have told you is not true."

"Thank you for suggesting so admirable a reference respecting your character as this convenient friend would doubtless be," the Colonel, looking anything but grateful, rejoined.

"Ah! now you are speaking unkindly of poor Em. How can I make you believe that she has acted throughout from motives of the purest kindness?"

"Do you call it pure kindness on the part of a girl older and more experienced than herself to assist a mere child to correspond clandestinely with a scoundrel? No, Florence, I will endeavour to forget your juvenile folly, and even the want of confidence which you have shown towards myself, but as regards your friend, you must give her to understand that she can no longer be a guest of mine."

"But how can I tell her that she is to go? I promised her that you would be convinced, when I had told you all, that she, at least, is blameless."

"You may tell her, if you like, that I am less credulous than you expected to find me," said Sir Wilfred; and he was preparing to leave the room, when Florence, approaching nearer, said, in a tone that was rendered pathetic by the tearfulness of its entreaty,—

"But you will not hurry her away? You will give her time to write to London and prepare her relations for her return? Wilfred, dear," she added, gaining courage from his silence, and venturing to lay upon his arm a timidly-detaining hand, "it is not like you to be so hard, so unforgiving towards a girl whose only fault it is that she has shown herself too blindly faithful towards your wife."

Poor Florence! Had she expended her last sleepless night in search after the most expedient fashion in which to appease the anger of her husband, she could hardly have hit upon one less likely to succeed. The idea that any act on the part of *his* wife could have been of so *shady* a character as to call, in her behalf, for the exercise of Miss Vidal's powers as a confidante and scapegoat, was as gall and wormwood to the proud spirit of the indignant husband, and his reply was in accordance with his feelings.

"Let her telegraph to her friends that there is scarlet fever, or diphtheria, whichever complaint she most fancies, in the house; only bear in mind that not another night must she sleep under my roof."

The uselessness of further striving in her friend's cause being now thoroughly apparent, Florence ventured to murmur a few words in her own behalf.

"And you do forgive me? And you

will trust me as you did before?" she said meekly.

Her small hands were clasped in prayer, and her face was very lovely in its deep humility, yet her husband's only response to her petition was simply the uncompromising words,—

"I will strive my utmost to forget."

CHAPTER II.

WAR TO THE KNIFE.

FLORENCE GREGORIE was the reverse of a strong-minded woman, and consequently the task of informing her friend that, according to Sir Wilfred's fiat, she, the hitherto apparently welcome guest, must perforce take her departure from Royalty Square, was, to her thinking, anything but an enviable one. Her nature partook essentially of clinging elements, and although the good opinion which of Em's principles and feelings she had entertained had been of late sensibly modified, the idea of giving that young person pain, greatly distressed her. There was, however, no possible means of escape from the ordeal that was imposed upon her, and it was therefore with a heavy heart that she knocked at her friend's door, and listened to the " Come in " which, to her appeal for admittance, was the prompt response.

She found Miss Vidal busily engaged in the, to her, congenial task of altering and improving a favourite dinner-dress, in order that it might meet the requirements of a ballroom, and the sight of her occupation did not tend to decrease the perturbation of Lady Gregorie's spirits. She remembered, with a pang, that the preparations on which Em was engaged had in view a certain all-im-

portant festivity which, in the shape of a
County Town Ball, was to be given in
honour of a Royal Prince; and that to
the said ball Miss Vidal, under the
chaperonage of her friend, looked forward with eager anticipations of pleasure
to being present. That these anticipations of enjoyment must inevitably
now be crushed, struck a chill on her
entrance into Flo's kind heart a chill
that increased in intensity when her
guest, making way for her amongst
the mass of dismantled finery with
which the chairs and sofa were laden,
said, with an embarrassed smile,—

"I hope you won't be hurt, dear Flo,
by the transmogrification which your
kind present is undergoing. It was so
awfully sweet of you to give me this
dress, that it goes to my heart to make

a change in it; but I could think of no other way of making myself fit to be seen on the twenty-ninth, save the utilising of your lovely gift. You will forgive me?" she added caressingly; "but I need not ask, seeing that you are always goodness itself to your poor hard-up friend."

These trusting words went nigh to bringing tears of remorse to the eyes of Florence Gregorie. A sense of guilt in that by her had been accepted the cruel task of inflicting dire disappointment on her friend, rendered her for a few moments silent. Nor was it until Em, surprised by her visitor's silence, made a tender inquiry after her health, that the latter said gently,—

"Thanks, dear. No, I am quite well. It is sorrow which makes me look, as I suppose I do—deplorable ; for I have come on a wretched errand, and can only hope you will believe that, in obeying my husband's commands, I do what is most distasteful to myself. Sir Wilfred is, as you know, a very determined man, and when he told me that—oh, dear Em, I cannot bear to say it!" and with tears gathering in her eyes, Lady Gregorie found her power of speech temporarily desert her.

Now in the matter of patience, the store possessed by Emily Vidal was far from being a goodly one, and therefore it is not surprising that when, at the very moment of an evidently important crisis, the strength of Lady Gregorie's feelings stood in the way of an expected *dénouement*, the young lady's temper should have risen within her at the delay. For a passing moment her habitual caution, and the rules of expediency which she had laid down for herself, were forgotten, and she said, in a voice which absolutely, from its abnormal sound, startled her hostess,—

"Nonsense! What is there that you cannot say to me? Have I not taken all your past peccadilloes upon myself? And, in order to save you from the anger of your stupidly jealous husband, have I not allowed him to think that I and not his wife had fallen under the spell of Major Brereton's attractions? Surely, after such sacrifices on my part as these, you can find no difficulty in speaking openly to me. What is it, pray, that Sir Wilfred has shown himself to be so determined about? Does he, or do you, wish me to humble myself still further? However, dear Flo, great as is my affection for you, I must tell you honestly that I will not own to having originated the idea of the diamond bribery."

"Nor," exclaimed Florence impetuously, for the tone taken by her quondam friend was one which her spirit was too high to brook with patience, "will the doing so be required of you. Sir Wilfred, I regret to say, has bidden me to tell you that your visit, which has afforded me so much pleasure, must come to an end, and that—"

"I am to go at once. Is that what your hospitable autocrat requires of me? If so, you may tell him from me that I will not submit to such an indignity. I must have time to prepare my people for my leaving Broadmere.

Surely, if he has any gentlemanly feeling, he will not send me out of his house as if I were a scullery-maid who had forfeited her character. However, before discussing that matter, perhaps you will give me some information as to what led to the resolution on Sir Wilfred's part of which you have just given me notice?"

Lady Gregorie, being, unfortunately for herself, possessed of a highly-emotional temperament, had been too much hurt and surprised by the behaviour of her guest, to regain immediately her wonted calmness of speech. For Miss Vidal's question, moreover, she was unprepared, and she therefore waited for a few moments to recover herself, ere she said, with as much composure as she could assume,—

"It was after an interview with Captain Leycester that Sir Wilfred questioned me so closely regarding our former acquaintance with Major Brereton that I could not do otherwise than answer truthfully the interrogations which he put to me. I hope you will believe that, both on your account and my own, I suffered much in speaking openly of the painful facts regarding which I was so closely questioned; but what could I do? there was nothing for me but to tell the truth."

"And did you make no effort," cried Em excitedly, "to save me from this bitter humiliation? Did you allow that courteous husband of yours to treat me —without a remonstrance on your part —as a woman whom he could with impunity outrage and insult?"

" Indeed, dear Em, I was not so un-
grateful. I reminded Wilfred of your
generous act in taking my follies upon
yourself, and entreated him not to inflict
such severe pain either upon you or
upon me as he seemed resolved on
doing."

" And what was his reply ? " demanded
Miss Vidal, as, with an air of studied
calmness, she confronted the woman
(*friend* as she truly felt no longer) whose
superior social position had long been
to her a source of envy, and from whose
house she was about to be banished in
disgrace. " Your pleadings," she continued bitterly, " could not have been
very earnest ones, since they had no
effect upon Sir Wilfred's resolve concerning me ; while, as regards yourself, I
conclude that, after making due confes-

sion of your faults, you are restored to favour, and may hereafter flirt with impunity with any of the good-looking young fellows who send you bouquets of hothouse flowers, and worship you as a divinity."

This last taunt proved too much for Lady Gregorie's patience to endure with calmness. The sense, too, of her own powerlessness (the mute evidence of her innocence having been destroyed) to reinstate herself in her husband's good opinion, lent added poison to the bitter words which had flowed so unexpectedly from Emily Vidal's tongue, and it was consequently with a thoroughly aroused sense of injustice that she said angrily,—

"You have no right, Em, to speak to me in this disrespectful manner. I have always, as you must well know, been ready to prove myself your friend—"

"Always," sneered Em, "when you were in a scrape, and were in want of a cleverer head than your own to help you out of it. So much, at anyrate, I am willing to acknowledge."

"I am sorry that your memory is so short," retorted Florence, whose indignation was naturally increased by every fresh proof of her guest's ingratitude which issued from that young person's lips. For almost every article of furniture which the room contained bore witness (in the shape of rich silks and costly laces) to the fact of "benefits forgotten" now, of Lady Gregorie's generosity towards her impecunious friend ; nor did that friend find it altogether easy, whilst standing in the midst of those surroundings, to carry herself with a bold and unblushing front before the woman whom she had begun to hate. That "they ne'er pardon who have done the wrong," is a truth of which few who have had personal experience of the heart's "desperate wickedness" can entertain any doubt; and Florence did not, perhaps, form a too uncharitable judgment of Miss Vidal's feelings towards herself, when she added, with icy coldness of manner, " But, until you have succeeded in drawing a veil over the past, perhaps you will not be sorry to hear that my chances of domestic happiness are effectually blighted. The destruction of those horrible letters was a fatal step. Without them, I have no chance of persuading Sir Wilfred of my innocence, and I must live henceforward under the shadow of his suspicion and displeasure."

It had been far, poor woman, from her intention, when she commenced her indignant protest, to lay bare, as she had done, her most sacred and hidden griefs to the inspection of her companion; but, like all impulsive and tender-hearted women, the sympathy of her kind was as necessary to her as the air she breathed. It had hitherto been her wont, when a crumpled rose leaf (rare occurrence! for her life was a singularly happy one) chafed the moral cuticle of the Colonel's light-hearted wife, to repose in Em's sympathising breast her passing troubles, and it was as much from force of habit as from the rush of self-pity which surged within her, that the imprudence of which she had been guilty was owing. The voice, always gentle and low, of the unhappy wife, had trembled audibly as she made her plaint, and her distress of mind was so evident, that Em, possibly gathering for herself hope for the future from the sorrows of her friend, changed her tactics, and, in a more conciliatory tone, remarked :—

"The destruction of the letters was certainly a foolish act on your part; still, I cannot but hope that your assurances, backed by mine, will have weight with Sir Wilfred. You will try your influence again, will you not, dear Flo? Only fancy the shame, the disgrace, of being turned in this summary fashion out of doors! And then there are my own people! What may they not imagine has happened to cause a scandal so every way

frightful? They are particularly hard up
too just now, moreover, for my father,
who, as I have told you, is never con-
tented to remain long in one place, has
taken it into his head to give up the
Maida Vale house, and remove his family
to the scene of his horse-breeding. These
moves of his are absolutely ruinous, and
if I am to be, as a climax, thrown back
unexpectedly on their hands, the row
will be something awful to contemplate.
Could you not gain even a fortnight's
reprieve for me, dear Flo?" she added
coaxingly, "if it could be only until after
the Town Hall affair, which they know at
home that I have looked forward to so awfully, I should be eternally grateful. You
will plead again for me, won't you, dear?"
and, greatly to Lady Gregorie's distress,
she sank upon her knees, and looked up

with imploring eyes into those of the
visitor into whose ears she had lately
poured spiteful and insulting words.

The silent head-shake with which her
entreaty was met did not prove immediately effectual, emphatic although it
was, in checking the torrent of Miss
Vidal's words. That young person had
long since been of the opinion—one
which she had read in some English
translation of a French novel—that "the
impossible is always possible for those
who wait and hope," and therefore, forti-
fied by this conviction, she still, whilst
holding Lady Gregorie's small shaking
hands in her own more muscular fingers,
continued her eager solicitations for a
respite.

"You cannot really mean," she said
imploringly, "that, as your silence

seems to imply, I am to go at once?
Think, dear, of the ignominy I should
have to undergo. How could I face
your servants? How bear up against
the contempt and ridicule which
I should read in their faces; and
how—"

"Oh, Em!" exclaimed Florence pity-
ingly, whilst the tears streamed from
her eyes, and she pressed with the
warmth of returning affection Em's hands
between her own, "do not, I pray
you, continue to torture both yourself
and me with these unavailing entreaties.
You have not now to learn how un-
changeable are at times Sir Wilfred's
resolves; and I dare not—I really dare
not—in this case act contrary to his
wishes. So now, my poor Em," she continued, as her companion sprang to her

feet and threw herself, unmindful of the finery she was crushing, on a chair, "let us consult together as to what is best to be done. The time allowed to us is unfortunately terribly short; but as Sir Wilfred suggested telegraphing—"

"*Sir Wilfred suggested!*" almost screamed Miss Vidal, as she pushed away her chair, and confronted her gentle visitor with furious looks. "And am I expected," she continued, in a voice that was absolutely hoarse with passion, "to obey the commands of a man who is, I must take the liberty of saying, no gentleman, or he would never dare to treat a lady who is temporarily under his protection as he is treating me?—for I conclude, from your mention of a telegraphic message, that

I am expected to leave Broadmere to-night."

"Exactly," rejoined Florence coldly, for she was again, in consequence of Em's impertinent remarks concerning Sir Wilfred, undergoing one of those mental reactions against her former friend to which, from the commencement of their somewhat stormy interview, she had been liable. It was, in fact, high time, considering the state of mind into which both ladies were wrought, that the closure of the debate should be put in force. Miss Vidal, being of a combative nature, would gladly have had what she called her "say" *out;* but Florence was very differently constituted, and her agitation and sorrow having culminated in a severe headache, she ardently longed for such rest of mind as in the quiet of her own room she could hope to enjoy.

Notwithstanding the occasional weaknesses of character of which in these pages Lady Gregorie has given proofs, she was quite capable, when circumstances compelled her to exertion, of making herself both respected and obeyed. This power she exerted now. Gently, but nevertheless very firmly, she gave Miss Vidal to understand that immediate steps for her departure from Royalty Square must be taken; and Em, although in her heart she hated, as only an envious and slighted woman knows how to hate, the *ci-devant* friend whose generous kindness had never failed her, busied herself mutely and sullenly in the work of preparation. Acting on Sir Wilfred's suggestion, a telegram announcing her advent was despatched to Sussex Road, Maida Vale; and Em, after partaking of an early but substantial dinner, was conveyed by Lady Gregorie in her victoria in time for the 6·30 train from Broadmere Station to London.

"Do not think of me with unkindness, dear," said kind-hearted Florence, as the carriage in which the quondam friends had, in days gone by, taken many a pleasant drive, bowled away from the Square, and truthfully, as Em concluded, from the sneering comments of the "pampered menials" who watched its departure. "Gladly would I have stood between you and this miserable mode of leaving us; but there are times—"

"Oh, never mind," interrupted Miss Vidal pettishly. "The less said about the past the better, only it will act as a warning to me never in future to take anybody's part. As for you, if you can feel happy after the way you have sacrificed me to your own selfish interests, all I can say is that I wish you joy of your want of heart."

"Hush!" whispered Florence, in a shocked and eager tone. "Do not talk so loud. The coachman will hear you, and— But here we are, thank Heaven! at the Station, and I need no longer listen to your unkind and most unjust reproaches."

The parting was, as may be supposed, as cold on both sides as parting could well be, and a few minutes later Em was left to reflect, in bitterness of spirit, on the "*ahs*" and "*ohs!*" of wonder with which on her return she would be greeted ; whilst Florence reflected, with the heaviest heart she had ever yet known, on the grievous, and, as she feared, irremediable loss of her husband's love and trust.

CHAPTER III.

EM THROWS LIGHT ON THE MATTER.

THE train from Broadmere by which Emily Vidal was expected did not as a rule reach London till twelve o'clock at night, yet, late as was the hour, and although for economy's sake the motto of "early to bed" was habitually practised in the Vidal household, every member of the family, stirred by the general curiosity to learn the cause of Em's unexpected return, was up and in readiness to receive her. Mrs Vidal, a faded and

over-worried woman, one of whose worst
misfortunes in life it had been that her
great-grandmother was the daughter of a
Marquis, insisted on the keeping up in
their impoverished establishment a very
faint imitation of what she believed to
be one of the daily habits of the "great."
For instance, half-an-hour previous to
the "laying" by a "house-parlour-maid"
of an often-used dinner-cloth, the feeble
tinkle of a bell was at the hour of
seven P.M. heard, and forthwith the
females of the family disappeared to
their respective *toilettes*, thence shortly
to reappear in other, although probably in shabbier garments than those
for which they had been exchanged.
The head of the household, a good-
tempered, devil-may-care individual, whose
career in a cavalry regiment had been

cut short by debt, and who had since carried on a precarious and not very creditable existence as a "gentleman rider," was—a not unfrequent habit of his—absent from home. His breeding establishment in the neighbourhood of Aldershot—albeit it was not carried on in an extensive scale—called for constant supervision, and this was the more necessary, seeing that *Captain* Vidal, as he elected to be called, had lately taken to himself that not always desirable business agent popularly known as a partner; this fact also, together with the approaching migration of the family to Heather Lodge, was far from lessening the appearance of discomfort and untidiness in the midst of which it was the normal habit of the Vidal family to live and move and have their being.

"Well, we *are* a disreputable-looking lot," remarked the eldest girl, whose name was Hilda, and who had taken possession of a rocking-chair, the appearance of which was (from long usage) so much against it, that it had been pronounced in family conclave to be not worth the expense which sending it to Heather Lodge would entail; "and, mother," she shouted, for the maternal parent was a sufferer from deafness, an affliction which, on the part of her daughters, called for considerable vocal exertion, "do try and go to sleep. You will know about Emily soon enough; and if you don't get something of a night's rest, you will never be able to-morrow for the bother of flitting."

The Vidals were on the whole both a good-natured and an attached family, and, seeing that Mrs Vidal was one of the most tiresome and exacting of human beings, it may be counted for righteousness in her daughters, that, when ineffectually endeavouring to beat into their parent's "good ear" facts with which it was advisable that she should become acquainted, they rarely, on discovering that the case was hopeless, were guilty of losing their tempers. Even Emily, who was the least patient of the quartette, would strive, to the best of her ability, to hide her natural irritation when Mrs Vidal, with the tautology which is one of the most trying infirmities of old age, enlarged, as was her wont, on the greatness of her maternal descent, and boasted of the cousins who, in very truth, proved *distant* ones to her. As regarded Captain Vidal, his wife's deafness troubled him not at all. He had long since arrived at the philosophical conclusion that "what can't be cured must be endured," and therefore, when Mrs Vidal's unfortunate surdity rendered her incapable of catching the meaning of his words, it was his wont to turn over the task of making her understand to one of his daughters (Linda, the third girl, by preference) with the cheerful-sounding parental order of—

"You tell your mother what I mean, Lin," and forthwith that young person, whose place at table was at Mrs Vidal's side, and who was well accustomed to the duty which had devolved upon her, shouted into the ear of the afflicted one some wholly unimportant remark, which the lady of the house, jealous of her

wifely privileges, had, from the motion of
her husband's lips, and the direction of
his small, beady eyes, rightly decided
that he had addressed to her.

And this was the household to which
Emily Vidal, after her lengthened visit in
Royalty Square—a visit during which she
had indulged to her heart's content in
the luxuries which to the wealthy are as
the mere necessaries of life—was momentarily expected to return. But for the
element of curiosity which it had aroused,
the receipt of Emily's telegram would
hardly have awakened in the breasts of
her sisters any sensation of pleasure.
Linda, the only one of the four who had
never experienced the gnawing pangs of
envy in that Em had been, by means of
Lady Gregorie's friendship, exalted above
her fellows, was conscious of a certain

amount of nervous tremor when the time
when Emily's coming would, by the ring
of a cabman at the door, be announced.
Linda's health had never been strong,
and being of an imaginative turn of
mind, she had conjured up reasons for
her sister's sudden return, which had
rendered her last night a sleepless one,
and caused her to listen, as though in a
dream, to the loudly-spoken suggestions
of her elders regarding the possible
reasons for Em's abrupt return.

"What in the world can it be?" exclaimed for the hundredth time since the
arrival of the telegram, the oldest and
most inquisitive of the waiting ones;
whilst Bertha, the beauty of the family,
threw out a hint which Miss Vidal, eager
for a sensation, immediately took up and
mentally commented upon.

"I wonder," Bertha said, "whether her coming back can have anything to do with papa's new partner, Major Brereton. He was, you know, in the Chalkshire Rifles, and—"

But at that moment a cab—not a hansom, for Em's "plunder" was far too bulky for conveyance in even the roomiest of those far preferable vehicles—drew up drowsily to the door, and a loud ring at the bell from a breathless "runner," announced the fact that Miss Emily Vidal had arrived.

She looked, on her entrance, very wan and weary, and as the girls pressed forward to bestow upon her a sisterly embrace, her response to their greetings was the reverse of fervent. On seeing, by the light of a solitary and ill-burning lamp, that her mother had not yet retired to rest, a deeper shade of annoyance passed over Emily's face. There was no help for her now. Late as was the hour, and weary as were both her head and limbs, she must now give voice to the fictitious reason for her return which, during the journey, she had concocted; and, in her present condition of mind and feeling, she positively shrank from the ordeal of shouting into her mother's ear the falsehood which, when still unspoken, had not struck her as being so very black.

Mrs Vidal was the first to enter into the subject which, during twelve mortal hours, had absorbed the interests of the assembled family. She was wide awake now, and ready to be put *au courant* of the event, whatever it might be, which had restored the long-absent Emily to the bosom of her family.

"Well, my dear," the old lady said briskly, for the forty winks during which no sound broke the spell of her slumbers had tended greatly to her refreshment, "here you are again! And after such a surprise too! I declare I never was more startled than when I read your telegram. They are nasty things at all times, but when it comes to their telling you nothing at all, but just what makes you worry, worry, worry for something more, I, for one, had rather have been without one."

Em had drawn a rush-bottomed chair close to her mother's side, and having brought her pallid lips into near contact with the old lady's cap-frill, she spoke— for the benefit of the family in general— as follows :—

"You would hardly have thanked me

for sending you a longer telegram, for it is a case of threatened scarlet fever which has brought me away, and—oh, you needn't be frightened, I am quite safe not to do mischief. Little Freddie, the idol in Royalty Square, had a slight attack of fever, owing to drinking cold water when he was hot, and the first doctor who was called in having suggested scarlet fever, I thought it best, as the house is not large, and illness takes a great deal of room, to say that I would return home."

"And they were selfish enough to let you come away, and bring their fever to us!" exclaimed Hilda angrily. "I never heard anything so atrocious. I never thought much of your dear Lady Gregorie, but I could not have believed anything so bad of her as this."

"I don't see anything bad in it!" Em said stoutly. "Probably, although she was too well-bred to say so, Florence considered *me* selfish for proposing to leave her in her trouble. She could hardly press me to remain in an infected house, but I could see that she was hurt; for when a second doctor, the regimental one, came, and pronounced the child's ailment to be nothing worse than chicken pock, she did not urge · me to remain. She was, however, she said, very sorry for it all, and asked me to come and see them again when they were settled at St Margaret's."

Now seeing that Em's reputation for truthfulness did not stand especially high in her family, her explanation was taken *cum grano salis* by those to whom it was addressed, and, but for the lateness of the hour, it is probable that Hilda, who dearly loved to talk a matter out, would have indulged in further questionings regarding the subject on hand; but a remark from Em that she was "awfully tired," induced her to put off till the morrow any allusion which she had previously been on the point of making to her father's recently-adopted partner.

On the following morning, an opening for the introduction of Major Brereton's name into the domestic councils was unexpectedly made by Emily herself. The latter, finding herself the first, after her eldest sister's appearance, to enter the breakfast-room, said irritably,—

"What in the world is the reason of this sudden change? Surely for people as poor as we are, London is the best place?

We shall know no one at Heather Lodge but racing men and bookmakers; besides, the expense of moving will be awful."

"We shall know papa's new partner, I suppose," suggested Hilda. "He is a Major Brereton; and as he has only just left the Chalkshire Rifles, you probably met him at Broadmere?"

Hilda, who had inherited the sharp black eyes of her sporting parent, kept them fixed, as she waited for an answer, on her sister's face; and when the latter, with a rise of colour which she would have given much to conceal, replied, with an attempt at *insouciance*,— "Oh, yes, I knew him slightly. They did not like him in Royalty Square, so he was not often asked there," the crafty questioner felt well assured that between Major Brereton and Em there had been " passages " which, for the nonce at least, it did not suit Miss Emily's book to enter upon.

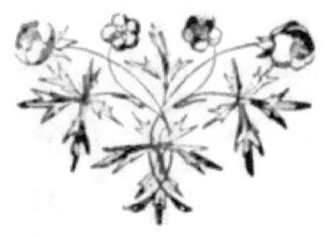

CHAPTER IV.

MRS DENHAM WRITES A LETTER.

GUY'S preparations for departure kept him so fully employed that several days elapsed before he found time to pay his promised visit to the "Shanty." Meanwhile, the idea that no court-martial would be held on Guy Leycester began to gain ground. He had, it could not be denied, committed a grave breach of discipline, but then the provocation to do so had been great. Major Brereton's character as a black sheep was becoming rapidly unfolded. Captain Leycester's interest at the Horse Guards was great, and he had volunteered for service abroad. Under these especial circumstances, therefore, his sword, was, with an "admonition," restored to him, and he was once more a free man.

Free! Yes, but to do what in life he most dreads, is, he knows, the first use which Duty demands him to make of liberty; for the truth must now, in all its entirety, be told to Gertrude, and his heart sinks within him at the bare thought of what, in the coming interview, both he and she are fated to undergo.

.   .   .   .

The husband of Gertrude Denham was not, as has already been hinted, an especially amiable man, and it had been with a certain amount of satisfaction that he had brought home to his wife the news of Captain Leycester's arrest. Although the time when he had loved Gertrude Annesley had long since passed away, he was still capable of feeling jealous of the man against whose attractions he felt persuaded she was not wholly proof, and it was with much exaggeration that he informed her of the heavy blow which Guy had dealt to his adversary, and of the danger of death, for as such he described it, in which the wounded man was lying.

"It will be a case of manslaughter against Leycester, if the man dies," he said; and Mrs Denham's state of mind as she listened to this surmise, is easier to imagine than to describe. Her distress and anxiety, were, however, not of long duration. The report that Major Brereton's injuries were not likely to cause much sorrow to any friends whom he might happen to possess, speedily got abroad. Suspicions also of his inculpation in regard to the diamond robbery began to be whispered about, and these rumours were soon followed by the release of Guy Leycester from durance vile.

Gertrude's joy, when again she looked upon the face of the man she loved, was checked by the expression of sadness which was so plainly visible on his countenance.

"Oh, Guy," she cried, "what a most miserable week we have gone through! And now—now I fear that there is some fresh trouble. Is it so? Tell me quickly, for I cannot bear that you should have anxieties which I do not share."

"Dear Gertrude," he answered gently, "I wish—oh, how I wish—that you were less good and kind. For my anxieties are all for you,—you whom I have dragged into a sort of partnership with my miserable debts,—you whom I must leave—"

"*Leave!*" she repeated, with a short sharp cry of anguish. "Oh! what shall I do? What good will my life do me if you go away? My husband said something which I fancied meant —but I thought that it was only to torment me — that you were going to exchange. And where are you going? and when? You spoke once of the Soudan, but I cannot believe that you could be so cruel. Guy, dearest, I am only your friend, I know, but I think that I deserve your confidence. Is there any truth in the report that Miss Malcolm has—oh, I cannot bear to think of it! She is very rich, but you would not be happy with her—"

"Nor have I any intention of trying to be so," Guy rejoined. "No, dear, I am not thinking of such a very desperate step as that; I have only, as I before told you, volunteered, by way of variety, for the Soudan—"

"And are you really going there? Oh! Guy," and she sank back, pale as a corpse, in her chair, "it sounds to me like death—"

"Whilst to me," he, endeavouring to speak lightly, said, "it sounds only like deliverance. If it were not for you,—

you, dear, generous woman, I should feel nought but joy. It is the knowledge that I have been the means of causing the voice of slander to be busy with your name, which weighs upon my conscience, and causes me to obey the call of duty with a heavy heart. If I should not return—"

"If you do not return," she said, speaking with closed eyes, and like one in a dream, "my death will make everything smooth and easy. For I cannot live without sometimes seeing you. My home is too miserable, and I feel that my trials are greater than I can bear."

"Do not speak so despondingly dear," said Guy; and as he pressed her two cold hands in his, it comforted for a moment this poor weak woman to *feel* that in that lengthened pressure there was something closer than a mere friendly feeling. "You must look at the bright side of things, and hope that I may come back to you a wiser and a better man."

She was silent, passing over in mental review the many dangers to which the man for whom she had sacrificed so much was about in that cruel Soudan war, to be exposed. On the increased home misery which she would herself, were his precious life to be cut short, incur, she could not choose but dwell, and now that she was about to lose the support and comfort of his daily visits, her own loss of self-respect in that she had allowed herself not only to love, but to betray her feelings towards one whom to dote on was a sin, filled

her with the deepest shame. And if
he should share the fate of the many
brave men whose bones lay buried in
that distant land, what, save bitterest
remorse for the past, would be hence-
forth her portion? Whilst for him—for
the dear one who might be cut off in
his sinful, thoughtless youth, what could
she dare to hope? During the period
when her love for Guy Leycester had
been growing into a passion, the
strength of which she found it difficult
to conceal, she had, without much difficulty, succeeded in banishing from her
mind all thoughts of that other world
to which, in the days when she had
been conscious of no guilty imaginings,
her musings had so often tended. She
had been wont, in that season of com-
parative innocence, to turn for comfort

to the blessed hopes held out in Holy
Writ to those who in this dark world
are troubled and sore smitten; and
now, when her fears for Guy grew
black within her, the thought of his un-
fitness to meet his Judge gave her courage
to say abruptly, but with nevertheless a strange solemnity of manner,—

"Guy, dear, do you ever—forgive
me for asking you such a question—
remember that there is another world
than this? Do you ever ask of God
to forgive your sins? It would be so
terrible to die unpardoned, and we
have all—I especially—need of forgiveness;" and as, in broken accents,
she breathed her timid warning, she
passed her hand caressingly over the
brown, closely-cut hair of the hitherto
thoughtless soldier, whose handsome

head, for he was seated on a stool beside her, was bending low over her knees.

Guy's sensations on hearing these startling questions were the reverse of enviable. In common with, I greatly fear, the majority of men of his age and class, he had as completely forgotten the existence of an All-seeing God as if he had never in his boyish days been taught the awful truth that the commission of evil deeds will not go unpunished. But he could not confess this fact to Gertrude, neither could he own to her that were he to look closely into his inmost mind, he would find there but little of the faith in prayer which in her was so strong and comforting.

His silence, the result, not, as she

feared, of annoyance, but of a sense of
the false position in which he found
himself, greatly distressed his companion, but, having ventured so far to
probe his conscience, she would not
yield weakly to her fears, but said, in
her soft, pleading voice,—

"Will you promise me one thing,
Guy?"

"Anything," he answered eagerly.
"Only tell me what I can do to give
you pleasure."

"Promise me then," she said, and the
tears, as she breathed her prayer fell
down her colourless cheeks like rain,
"that if you should be in deadly peril,
you will say in your heart one fervent
prayer to God for mercy. Promise me
this, dear, and then I too may hope,
when I have obtained, through repentance,

pardon for my past sins, to meet you again in heaven."

Mechanically, and as though acting in simple obedience to a wish of hers, he gave the required promise, but if the trusting woman could have looked into his heart, she would have read there a protest against the concession he had made ; for Guy told himself (nor can we deny that he spoke, to his inner consciousness, the truth) that Prayer delayed until the hour of peril comes, is the action of a coward, and that, being such, can be of little avail to the etitioner. Not, however, for any consideration that could be offered him, did he feel able to increase poor Mrs Denham's too evident unhappiness by a confession that his faith was less steadfast than her own, and therefore he, after

giving the required promise, limited himself to saying, with heartfelt fervour,—

"God bless you, dear, you have been,
and are still, my guardian angel. If I
had had a different mother,—one who
had talked to me as you have done, I
might, perhaps, have been less of a
curse both to myself and others. People
talk of a fellow being no one's enemy
but his own, but my experience tells
me that a man cannot avoid, whilst
making an utter fool and selfish monster of himself, dragging others into the
pitfalls which are yawning to engulf
him."

"Poor fellow!" Mrs Denham, with a
vigorous endeavour to recover herself, exclaimed. "You must follow the advice
which you have given to me, and hope
for better things. You are still so young,

that—" but interrupting herself, for she
dreaded a renewal of agitation which she
was powerless to check, she added,—
"But tell me you will not go immediately. There must be so much for you
to do—"

"Ah, there you are mistaken. If *I*
am not in light marching order, I do
not know who is. To-morrow I must
run up to town to see my people, and
show myself to the authorities; but I
shall return the day after, and report
progress to you."

Gertrude's heart sank within her, but
she did her utmost to seem brave, as
she said tremulously,—

"Then this is not good-bye. I shall
see you again, shall I not? before you
leave me quite."

"Of course you will," was Guy's cheerfully-sounding answer. "This is only an *au revoir* dear friend; and we will say it now, for I have to see the Colonel, and there are letters which I am obliged to write."

And so it came about that the parting of those two who were destined never in life to meet again, was, in appearance, as calm and unemotional as though they had been about to see each other on the morrow, and discuss, with no fear of impending evil hanging over their heads, the topics of the day and hour. But this is forestalling events which must now, in their regular course, be narrated.

After Guy Leycester's departure, Mrs Denham kept her spirits from sinking to zero with the hope, that on the following day but two he might be able to spare her a few minutes of his now valuable time; but the weary hours sped by, and he who had become, to her own exceeding sorrow and remorse, the very sunshine of her life, came not. Then arrived for her the weary night, during the long watches of which her inward and ceaseless cry was,—"Would God it were morning!" and then the heavy sleep of utter exhaustion, from which she awoke to find a letter lying on the coverlet. It had been opened by her husband, and in it she read these few but terrible words :—

"It grieves me to write that I cannot return to Broadmere. The troopship sails in two days, and I must be on the spot. Once more, farewell, and may God bless you.—Yours ever truly,

"Guy Leycester."

It was well for Gertrude Denham that at that crisis in her life the eyes of a husband jealous for the honour of his name were constantly upon her; for self-control became for the half-broken-hearted woman a matter of absolute necessity. Richard Denham was essentially a bully, and was well skilled in the art of ingeniously tormenting. Envy of Guy's great and universal popularity was rife within him. It was, he constantly reminded himself, a popularity and also a consideration so wholly undeserved, and one which he, who had always conducted himself as a man of honour and a gentleman—he who, small as was his income, had kept himself clear from debt, had utterly failed to win.

And now the man had gone,—gone to win, perhaps, more golden opinions from his fellow-men—and gone, it might be

—to die! Meanwhile, the tyrant husband, keeping, as I before said, his eye
upon his wife, amused himself by talking
in her presence, with affected concern, of
the perils and privations, the sickness and
the hardships, of England's little "army
of martyrs," and of watching on her mo-
bile face the effects of his carefully-
chosen words.

Truly thankful during those slowly
passing and most miserable days was
Gertrude in that she had not by any weak
yielding on her part to *Temptation* added
to the long array of guilt which she
greatly feared stood unrepented of, against
the man she loved. Of the lot of the two
women who, for widely - different causes,
had been deprived of the torturing consolation of farewell words with the departing
soldier, that of Gertrude Denham was in-

finitely the most pitiable. *Her* life was a worse than solitary one, whereas May, the darling of her home, was surrounded by loving hearts, and by those who strove by every means in their power to turn her thoughts from dwelling on the absent one. And again, Gertrude had never told her love. For her there existed no precious memories of tender love-passages. The "touch of a" now "vanished hand" had never caressed her shining hair, or been allowed to linger with sweet seductiveness within her own ; whereas May, child almost though she was, could luxuriate in fancy on not a few ecstatic memories. For her there had been, as also for her lover,—

> " Hearts beating,
> At meeting ;
> Tears starting,
> At parting."

And something akin to the self-congratulatory feeling that "Come what might she had been blest," supported her spirits during the first trying period of separation. Happily also for Guy's child sweetheart, she was still in the early springtime of existence. The blessed sap of Hope was rising in her veins, and acting as a tonic to strengthen her nerves for whatever added sorrow Fate might have in store for her; but for Gertrude Denham there was no such tonic possible. In the case of a childless woman, and a wife unloving as she is unloved, the future of the bereaved one (supposing always, as was indeed the case with Gertrude), she sets no value on the beauty and the charm of manner which Time has left untouched, is dark indeed.

A profound student of female nature

has, as the result of his experience, left
behind him the often-quoted axiom, that
" *Le remords est né de l'abandon et non
pas de la faute.*" Now Gertrude had
neither sinned nor had she suffered the
mortification of being abandoned; and
yet her remorse for the past was keen
indeed. She sorrowed in that she had
never allowed the man whose slightest
touch set her pulses throbbing, to know
how dear he was. He had gone, possibly to his death, and to the end he
had believed her to be cold of heart,
and unregardful of his love; and now a
great longing seized her that he should
at last learn the truth. In this world,
the chances were that they two would
never meet again; and so the weak, impulsive woman told herself that there could
be no sin in pouring out to him on paper

the story of her love, and of the fierce
battles against the temptations of her
own heart which she had waged. She
had begun her letter calmly, and with
something approaching to womanly reti-
cence and dignity; but the subject, her
heart being so deeply engaged in it, was
an all-engrossing one, and lo!

"Each word she wrote, Love turned to fire."

Far was the unhappy writer from
surmising that other eyes besides those
of the man to whom she wrote would
read her soul's outpourings, but so, alas
for her! it chanced. There came a
time, and that speedily, when the letter
which Gertrude Denham had in her
dreary solitude written to the man for
whose sake she had uncomplainingly
suffered wrong, fell into unfriendly

hands. When the heart of the chival-
rous soldier who would have championed
her innocence to the death had ceased
to beat, his sisters, true to the instincts
of a posthumous jealousy which, when
experienced in seasons of affliction, it
seems difficult to understand, had opened
the letter which had told him of poor
Gertrude's love, and from its pages had
chosen not only to draw conclusions which
were unfavourable to her character, but
had openly declared their belief in her un-
worthiness. It needed but this last drop
to fill to the brim the unhappy woman's
cup of misery; but the stern necessity
of keeping from her husband's knowledge
the fact that Guy Leycester had been
more to her than the mere acquaintance
which, in the presence of her tyrant,
he had seemed to be, enabled her, out-

wardly at least, to bear her cross
without any betrayal of her inward
suffering. Truly her heart, and that
alone, knew its bitterness, and of joy
there was in future for Gertrude Denham
none in which a stranger could inter-
meddle !

CHAPTER V.

HOW THE LION DIED.

"IN the midst of *Death*, we are in *Life*." During every moment as it swiftly passes by a human soul returns to Him who gave it, and the feeble wail of a newly-born infant breaks upon its mother's ear. Whether the joining in wedlock of, it is to be hoped, some happy pairs, is an event of as frequent occurrence as are those of births and deaths, I am not prepared to say, the above slightly tampered with quotation being simply the result of reflections on a scene of gaiety to which I am about to introduce the reader, the said scene of gaiety being in striking contrast to that which, in far-away Soudan, is being enacted.

The departure of Guy Leycester to the seat of war, and the grief, not loudly expressed, but nevertheless very deep and real, of the girl he left behind him, did not, as a matter of course, delay the preparations for Helen Durant's marriage. It was true that from the scene of one of the most cruel and indefensible of England's little wars, disastrous telegraphic intelligence might at any moment arrive,—true also was it that May's gentle heart was often racked with direst forebodings, and that her eyes, darkened by their long curled lashes, frequently showed signs of recent tears, yet, on the whole, the excitement attendant on the wedding arrangements produced a sensible improvement in her spirits.

As Helen's only bridesmaid, her own dress became an object of interest only secondary to that which she took in Nellie's bridal costume, and the question of whether her "nun's veiling" costume should be relieved by pink or blue was discussed by her with an amount of animation from which Mrs Durant drew cheerful auguries for the future.

"I really think," the pretty young creature said, as she, with her golden head on one side, and her dark blue eyes fixed upon the rival colours, endeavoured to arrive at a conclusion, "that pink will be the most effective. What do you think, Elphy?" she continued, addressing her brother-in-law elect. "Which shall I look best in—pink or blue?"

"Blue, decidedly," was the uncompromising reply. "It has long been an accepted fact that pink for girls of your colouring is inadmissible. Fair ones with golden locks must content themselves with blue; and be thankful," he added, with a smile, as he laid a brotherly hand on the young girl's shoulder, "that there is such a shade to set off their attractions."

He had no sooner spoken than he felt that there ran through the slender frame on which his strong hand lightly rested, a shiver, which was suggestive of internal emotion. Then the sweet carnation lips quivered, and those who watched and loved the girl, remembered that in the days gone by, when Guy Leycester was expected, May invariably contrived either to clothe herself in a cerulean-hued costume, or to bind her golden hair with a riband of the colour which her sweetheart most admired.

"Do you think she is as far as ever from forgetting him?" asked Mrs Durant, in a low, and deeply feeling voice, when the girl, unable to control her growing emotion, had silently left the room. "Even I recollected poor Guy's especial liking for blue; nor had I forgotten the pretty 'maiden snood,' as he used to call it, of pale blue riband, which, since he went away, she has never worn; and now —Well, poor child, I do not pretend to understand her, and she was once," with a melancholy smile, "as easy to be read as a child's hornbook!"

"And so she will be again, dear mother," rejoined Elphinstone consolingly; "she is going through a painful experience, but her youth is all in favour of the trial to which my thoughtlessness has exposed her, tending rather to her eventual good than to her injury. If I did not believe this, I should reproach myself still more severely than I do for not having taken better care of my little sister."

"Well, we must hope the best," rejoined the widow sadly, "but, in the meantime, I tremble to think of what the consequences might be to May if bad news of Captain Leycester were to arrive. As it is, she frets, I fear, when she is alone, at never hearing anything about him."

"Still," said Elphinstone, who had

caught sight of a white dress among the garden shrubs, and was preparing to join the lady of his love, "you think I am right, do not you, in making no allusion, in her presence, to Guy's letters?"

"Certainly. The less she dwells upon his memory the better. It seems a hard probation for her to go through, but, after all, to hear Captain Leycester's account to you of the dreadful unhealthiness of the camp at Suakim, and of the terrible chances of fever which our poor soldiers run there, would only make her more unhappy."

"Yes; what with the constantly-recurring night attacks, and the way the Arabs have of burying their dead only a few inches beneath the surface of the soil, our poor fellows are too heavily handicapped by contingent circumstances for a very large proportion of them to have a chance of fighting their battles over again."

"Poor fellows indeed," responded Mrs Durant, who, being a woman of strong religious convictions, was frequently not a little shocked by an absence of those convictions in her daughter's *fiancé.* "We can only give them the benefit of our prayers, and trust that Providence will watch over them by night and by day, and that both in their goings-out and their comings-in, their feet will not be suffered to slip."

Rowley Elphinstone allowed the widow's last remark to pass unanswered. A better and a more conscientious man than he did not, in the ranks of the British army, exist, but Faith had, in his idiosyncrasy, its limits, and, after the fashion of the First Napoleon, who professed a belief that Providence was always on the side of *les gros battalions*, he placed more reliance on a General who knew his business, and kept a good look-out, than on the longest prayers against battle and murder and sudden death that ever were breathed by man or woman.

The wedding was to be a very quiet one. Mrs Durant had, owing alike to the shortness of her purse, and her present disinclination for society, given little encouragement to callers at the cottage to repeat their visits, and, consequently, the invited guests consisted almost entirely of the clergyman of the parish whose office it was to make 'one flesh of pretty Helen Durant and her soldier lover, and of a few of the latter's intimates in the regiment; the Colonel and his wife standing, of course, first and foremost amongst the military whose presence on the occasion was requested.

"I wish, dear Nell, that there were more people coming to admire you," said May to her sister, when, on the occasion of a dress rehearsal, she stood admiringly by Helen's side before the cheval glass. "But there will be the band, and the soldiers of Elphy's company lining the aisle, which will be nice;" and May could hardly suppress a tear, as her thoughts flew back to the goodliest soldier of them all, who, instead of playing the part of groomsman to his friend (a *rôle* which on the programme had been his to perform), might even now be lying stark and cold upon the battle-field.

"I wonder," said Helen, who read

her sister's thoughts as in a book, and who lost not a moment in changing the conversation to a topic less suggestive than that of military bands and officers in the dark-green uniform of their Corps, whose expected attendance at the approaching ceremony had had the effect of filling May's sapphire eyes with tears, —" I wonder why Lady Gregorie does not say more positively whether or not she and Sir Wilfred will be present to-morrow. Her answer is so puzzling; and I feel sure that she wished to accept our invitation."

" Perhaps—" May was beginning, and then stopped suddenly, for she recollected that it was Guy who had laughed with her over the Colonel's dislike to encouraging matrimony amongst his officers; and although since her lover's departure a fortnight had elapsed, and albeit she had forgiven her mother for the part which the latter had played in defrauding her of a last farewell, the child could not as yet bring herself to speak lightly of the lover she had lost. " Perhaps," she said, whilst her colour came and went, " it is Sir Wilfred who, for some reason or other, objects. Elphy says that he has grown rather martinet-ish (whatever that may mean) lately, and, if so, and if he does not feel in the humour to be pleased, he had better remain away."

By this sample of little May's state of mind, it will be seen that she did not feel altogether in charity with the Colonel, whose dislike to his officers taking to themselves wives had become a matter of notoriety. Great allowances were at

this time made, and that especially by
her mother, for the waywardness which
the poor child was at this trying period
of her young life given to display; but
when, after much entreaty, permission was
at length given to her to add a few lines
to one of Rowley Elphinstone's frequent
letters to his late brother officer, a fit
of hysterics followed on the reaction of
joy which May after writing her tender
words to her absent lover experienced,
Mrs Durant bitterly repented of the concession she had made. There came, however, a time, and that shortly, when the
memory that Guy had, before the end was
reached, received the loving words which
she had indited, did good work in re-
conciling the bride-elect to the inevitable. We must not, however, anticipate
events which all too quickly sent a thrill

of horror throughout the length and breadth of England.

The wedding at Ivy Cottage was pronounced by all present to have been a "very pretty" one, and to have gone off remarkably well. The church in which the ceremony took place was old, and, like the cottage, ivy-clad. Its interior also was prettily adorned with flowers, for the proclivities of the Incumbent were Ritualistic, and he therefore considered it his bounden duty to spare the assistants not one syllable of the marriage service. It was, perhaps, as well, taking this circumstance into consideration, that during a portion of the ceremony the thoughts of the bridesmaid had been more with her own soldier love in the Soudan than even with the darling sister by whom, until of late, her every feeling had been shared.

When the ceremony was over, and the
bridal party had returned to the refreshment of a very simple breakfast, the
rector, Mr Manvers, congratulated Mrs
Durant in that the wedding had not
been a weeping one.

" Everyone behaved beautifully," he
said, " which," and here he bowed cour-
teously to the bride, " is, I hope, a
happy omen for the future."

" Oh, you need not praise Helen,"
laughed May; " she is constitutionally,
as the doctors say, dry-eyed. As for me,
I was only kept from tears by my fear
of doing damage to the lovely satin train
that lay in waves at my feet. There is
nothing like ' setting a resolution ' (you
remember dear old nurse's words, don't
you, mother?); well, I set a resolution,
and I never shed a tear."

"And you have your reward," the rector said gallantly, "in looking so fresh and bright; for, notwithstanding all that poets have said in praise of 'th' unanswerable tear,' there can be no doubt that beauty is not, as a rule, at its best when in the melting mood."

He did his utmost, that worthy, comfortable-looking "man of God," to make the long hour which the breakfast, and the usual compliments of the occasion, occupied, pass off pleasantly; but in the hearts of the chief actors on the stage, there existed an element of sadness which it was beyond his power to reach. The bride, dearly as she loved the man to whom her vows had just been plighted, fully realised, as her eyes fell upon the saddened faces of her mother and sister, the blank which her absence would occa-

sion in their little circle. She pictured
them to herself as (when the carriage
wheels which bore her away could be no
longer heard) shedding unavailing tears
for her loss; and Helen, one of the least
selfish of mortals, could almost have re-
proached herself in that she had had the
heart to bring this added sorrow on
their heads. Who amongst my readers
is either so fortunate or so heartless as
not to have experienced the strange mix-
ture of feelings which, when the moment
of an inevitable separation draws near,
prompts those who must of necessity be
left behind alternately to long for and
to dread the coming climax? It was
with antagonistic sensations such as these
that the about to be bereaved ones, who
were making brave efforts to seem bright
and happy, mentally contemplated the

dismal void which Helen's approaching
departure would leave in their loving
trio. They were trying moments.
Moments which *now* they would gladly
shorten, and which, anon, they would be
thankful, at almost any cost, to prolong.
It came at last, that painful parting,
and then, for Nature could no longer be
withstood, very plentiful were the tears
which the woman who was to be taken
away shed upon the tender bosoms of
those who must perforce be left to
grind at Life's weary mill without her.
The scene was cut short by the bridegroom, who, at the risk, as he whispered
to May, of being called a "brute,"
hurried his wife away.

"Come, darling, or we shall be late
for the Train," he said; and then he too
having affectionately kissed his newly-

made relations, the play was played out, the curtain fell, and two poor tired actresses were left alone in the "banquet hall" to mourn for one who was, as May, in the bitterness of her first sorrow said, "as good as dead" to them.

Poor little May! sorrow had, in truth, deeply shadowed the life which had once been so bright. She had had a lover, and such a lover! One in a thousand in his vocation, was the man who had won her heart, and left her mourning. A kind of military prestige had in the sunny days of Guy's brief courtship surrounded her. There was not a soldier of Captain Leycester's company who, when he saw the lady of their officer's choice pass by, abstained from saluting her; for, as I have before said, the men, with the keen instinct which enables soldiers to recognise a gentleman when they see him, both loved and revered their Captain. Their sorrow had been great when, driven by stress of circumstances, he left the old regiment, and betook himself, in search of glory, to the Soudan. Take him for all in all, they would never, they, with saddened faces, told each other, look upon his like again.

But the pretty smiles with which the "Captain's sweetheart" used to reward the men's salutes were never seen upon her sweet face now, and the sentimentally inclined amongst those gallant warriors were wont, with hushed voices, to speculate amongst themselves as to how, if the Captain never came back alive, his young lady would bear the news.

And all too soon it came—that dreadful telegram, which told to anxious, waiting England that, through causes which it is needless here to explain, British blood had been shed like water, and that it was owing to British valour, and to that alone, that a disaster only equalled by the massacre at Isandula had not been repeated on the sandy soil, and amongst the thick bushes of the Soudan.

.   .   .   .

It is the evening of the day when the disastrous telegram reached Broadmere, and every face at mess is shrouded in gloom, for the name of the quondam comrade, who had (despite his faults, or, it may perhaps be said, in part because of them) been dear to all, was foremost in the list of heroes who had given their lives to save their country's honour. Of course, the intelligence being telegraphic, but few particulars of the Action were given, but enough transpired to enable the officers to make a pretty shrewd guess that "someone had blundered" strangely. When the fuller details of the case became in some degree known, the wrath of these men of war was for a time unappeasable, and Rowley Elphinstone, who had returned from his brief honeymoon, was the most eager of all in his condemnation of the tactics in the Soudan which had brought the brave army to that terrible pass.

"There will probably be a Courtmartial," said Elphinstone; "but who will be run in it is impossible to say."

"Someone most likely deserves to be

shot," put in another Captain, whose name was Leigh, but whose voice, excepting on especial occasions, was rarely heard. "But I shouldn't wonder if, as so often happens, he meets with reward instead."

"What! after committing what seems to be the terrible blunder of camping in a thick jungle, and with a bush higher than a man's head, all round! Why, the veriest boy ensign would have known his business better!" rejoined Elphinstone, who, smarting severely under the double loss of British prestige and of his friend, struck so sharp a blow upon the mess - table that the glasses fairy shook upon the board.

"By heavens! what a scene it must have been!" exclaimed the Colonel. "The sudden cry of 'Stand to your arms, men! Stand to your arms!'

when hundreds, perhaps, of the poor fellows had no arms within their reach ; and then the rush of countless Arabs upon the little camp ! Ah— Well, if those fine fellows the Marines and the 49th Regiment hadn't succeeded, by dint of sheer discipline and pluck, in forming a Square, there would probably not have been a British soldier left to tell the tale."

" And what wonderful chaps, by Jove, those Arabs were to fight ! Even the women and children seem to have gone to the death for their country and their faith. I wish to God," continued Captain Leigh, whose ugly but sensible face was flushed with excitement, " that someone would correct those people who take a delight in running down these splendid fellows, and talking of them as if they were mere savages. Depend upon it, it is a base and shameful thing to run down a brave enemy, who took us all we knew to beat them."

"I warrant," said Elphinstone, and his lip quivered as he spoke, "that old Guy was in the thickest of the fight. His lungs were run through, you see, by an Arab spear, whilst he was rescuing a Marine from being trampled on by the overpowering rush of the Arab force. Well, he died the death he would have chosen, and now—"

"Let us drink," said Sir Wilfred, whose voice was hoarse from emotion, "to the memory of as brave a man, and as good a soldier, as ever wore a sword."

Then, all standing, and in solemn silence, those who had been Guy Leycester's comrades in life, drank to his memory in death. Slowly and sadly then they laid their glasses down, and left the dead hero enshrined in the hearts of those who, when he was amongst them, had to a man been proud to call him " friend."

.   .   .   .

On May Durant's grief, when the news that her lover had died a soldier's death was gently broken to her, it is best to draw a veil. Her sorrow was, as is the case with all deep afflictions, silent and uncomplaining, nor was she stricken down by one of those convenient fevers which novelists have ever at hand as a means, painful, it is true, and intensely trying to the spirits of the heroine's friends, of saving the reason of that young person from succumbing to the blow which had been dealt her. Amongst other blessings, May enjoyed that of being a thoroughly healthy girl. Born and bred in the country, she had yet to learn by experience that the fearful and wonderful threads called nerves (and which, by the way, are so closely allied to "feelings") exist in almost every human frame. Hysterical weakness was to the bereaved girl totally unknown, and although, during the early days of her great sorrow, she firmly believed in the reality of her wish to die, yet Time did by degrees its allotted work, and before twelve months had elapsed since her lover's death, May had begun to recognise the fact that Life had still something in it that was worth the living for. This recognition arose, of

course, in a great measure from the circumstance that the period when Guy
Leycester's charm of manner and ardent
wooing had opened for her the gates of
Paradise had been but short. The time
during which his image had filled her
heart with love's sweet rapture had
not been long enough to toughen the
fibres with which he had begun to
entwine himself round her heart, and
therefore as the days and weeks and
months wore on the said fibres relaxed
by degrees their hold, alike upon her
fancy and upon her feelings.

Mrs Elphinstone's return too produced
after a while a beneficial effect upon her
spirits. The honeymoon of the "happy
pair" had been cut short in consequence of the heartbreaking news which
had reached them from the seat of war.

There was no enjoyment for Helen whilst those she loved were in such deep grief at home, and Captain Elphinstone hungered (albeit he was taking his full of life's sweetest joys) to find himself with the brother soldiers of whose sympathy with his sorrow he felt so well assured.

The first tears which May, after the blow which had been dealt her, fell from her eyes, when they, on her brother-in-law's return, lighted on the dark green uniform which had once been, in their little drawing-room, a familiar and an ever welcome sight. The suggestion that he should not make his appearance in mufti emanated from Elphinstone, who said, when Helen expressed a fear that the sight of the well-known regimentals might be too great an ordeal for her sister to go through with safety,—

"Don't be alarmed, dear; what May wants is rousing, and if the old uniform can startle her into the relief which a flood of tears would bring, I for one shall consider that it has done excellent work."

And the result proved that he was right. May's burst of weeping relieved the oppression of her heart, and for the first time since her sore bereavement, she found courage to utter her dead lover's name. And from that day she appeared to find consolation in talking of him, and in listening to the praises of his bravery, and to the expression of deep regret which his early death had called forth. Early in the autumn the route for a change of quarters came, and when it was known that the Chalkshire Rifles were ordered to the Southern

coast, great was the satisfaction felt by
Mrs Durant, for Dr Brathwaite had
ordered change to the seaside for May,
and sanguine were the hopes entertained by those who loved her that the
Kentish breezes, together with novel
sights and sounds, would tend to the
recovery of this "stricken deer's" mental
health. During the autumn and winter,
May and her mother were the promised
guests of the newly-married pair. Captain Elphinstone was, as I have said, a
rich man, and they had therefore a
large house on the South Parade, so
that May could sit at her window facing
the sea, and watch the ever-changing
surface of the broad expanse of water.
And then there was the ever-moving
scene which along the gay Parade was
caused by the passing carriages and the

prettily-dressed maidens escorted, for the
most part, by gallant soldiers of the
Chalkshire Rifles, who looked, as probably was the case, as though love
whispers, tender as they were ephemeral,
were issuing from their lips.

And May Durant, seeing that it is
not in human nature to be always
fretting over past sorrows, awoke after
a while to a sense that existence might
yet become for her a pleasant thing.
She could never, she assured herself,
love again as she had loved the hero
sweetheart who lay buried in the
desert sand, but still— Well, to be
loved is very pleasant, and May, as
she watched the young girls smiling
on their soldier attendants as they
passed along the thronged parade,
heaved a sigh—was it one of harm-

less envy? at the sight, and loathed herself in that for a passing moment the possibility of being, in the days that were to come, ever false to the memory of her first love flashed across her brain.

CHAPTER VI.

CHARITY NEVER FAILETH.

A FEW days after the receipt
of the fearful intelligence from
Hasheen, Lady Gregorie was
surprised by the visit of an old
acquaintance, who had formerly been
engaged in doing three months' duty as
a curate at Broadmere. The Reverend
Edward Warburton, who was a distant
connection of the Gregories, was in
more respects than one a very young
man, and the curacy of St Gabriel's had
been his first charge. He had entered

upon that charge with the best inten-
tions, but his zeal in the cause in
which he put the most unbounded
faith, had not unfrequently landed him
ahead of discretion. In common with
many another juvenile apostle who had
done successful battle against temptation, Mr Warburton showed marked
intolerance towards those whose conduct had in the slightest degree laid
them open to suspicion.

In this respect he but followed the
example of his Rector, who, in his
lack of Christian charity, had even gone
the length of visiting Gertrude Denham in her home, and threatening her
that unless she confessed and repented
her of her past sins, he would not allow
of her presence at the Communion
table. This cruel and unjustifiable act,

when it came to Lady Gregorie's ears, roused within her breast an amount of indignation which she did not attempt to repress, and had it not chanced that at the period of its occurrence the Curate was absent on leave, she would, notwithstanding that her own domestic troubles were at that time weighing down her spirits, have given him the full benefit of her opinion regarding Mrs Denham's wrongs. However, *ce qui est differée n'est pas perdue*, and, as if in verification of the proverb, Mr Warburton had not been many minutes in Lady Gregorie's presence when she poured forth upon his head the vials of her wrath.

"I hope," she said, with an effort at calmness, although her fair cheeks flushed as she fired the first shot in defence of her injured sex, " that rumour said more than the truth when it accused you of being one with the Rector in the insult which he offered to Mrs Denham."

As Lady Gregorie's quick-sighted grey eyes took stock, from beneath their long lashes, of the Curate's few personal advantages, she made up her mind that had he been a more attractive-looking man, his judgments of others might be less severe than was reported to be the case. It was easy, Florence mentally decided, to be virtuous, when the individual who goes in for impeccability possesses light-hued, fish-like eyes, and the general effect of whose appearance is ill-calculated to win for him favour in the eyes of womankind. Lady Gregorie flattered herself (and that not without reason) that in such matters she was competent to give an opinion, and thus it chanced that, when on renewing her acquaintance with the Reverend Edward Warburton, she made up her mind that he more closely resembled a somewhat ill-conditioned Roman Catholic priest than a straightforward English gentleman; and it was this idea which encouraged her, ordained minister of the Gospel albeit her guest could claim to be, to visit him with the rod of her displeasure.

The Curate had taken a seat in front of the sofa which was occupied by his hostess. He had placed his broad-brimmed soft felt hat upon the knees of his somewhat well-worn nether garments, and the expression of his closely-shaven cheeks might be taken for that of one in whose breast a struggle for supremacy between the worship of Mammon and that of the Power under whose banner he had enrolled himself, was taking place. Lady Gregorie was a beauty, and, in his opinion, a fine lady, whom he preferred not to offend. Sir Wilfred also was the patron of three more, or less, desirable Livings, but, on the other hand, it was an object with him to keep on good terms with his present Rector, and to preserve, in Lady Gregorie's eyes, a character for consistency, and for an earnest desire to improve the morals of the Parish in which his present lot was cast. Under the pressure of these contending elements, it behoved him to be cautious, so, after a pause, he said,—

"I certainly agree with Dr Rogers in thinking that when a lady—a parishioner, either in Mrs Denham's or in any other station in life, has given occasion for evil reports of her conduct to be spread abroad, that it is the duty of her clergyman to give her warning of her danger."

"And to accompany that warning with a threat! Oh, Mr Warburton!" continued his excited interlocutrix, "was it on a mere suspicion of wrong-doing that Dr Rogers—a man, and therefore one who ought to be the protector, instead of the persecutor, of the weak— threw that monstrous stone at the unhappy wife of a bad and unkind husband? Do tell me," she, with increasing excitement continued, whilst the slender hands which rested on her lap were tightly clasped, "whether you clergymen ever remember the example of Him

who was born and died to show us
what in this short life should be our
rule of duty? There was something
more than ill-natured gossip regarding
the three erring women whom we read
of in the Scriptures, and yet when
the sinning ones were brought before
Him for judgment, had He aught but
forgiving words for those whom the
verdict of their fellow-sinners had pronounced, and perhaps justly so, to be
guilty, and deserving of punishment?
I am not acquainted with Mrs Denham
myself, for I believe that she lives a
kind of hermit's life, but the death of
poor Captain Leycester must have deeply
grieved her, and as one who must
acutely feel his loss, she has my
deepest sympathy."

"I was not aware," said Mr Warburton demurely, "that Mrs Denham and Captain Leycester were related."

"Nor indeed, I imagine, were they," rejoined Florence quietly. "But do you think it quite impossible for a woman, —one whose misfortune it is to have a brutal husband, to become warmly attached to a man who sympathises with her, and yet be pure in fa t as unsunned snow?"

The Curate's smile of incredulity whilst listening to Lady Gregorie's question was sorely trying to her patience, and still greater was her indignation when he said, slowly and superciliously,—

"I think you must admit, Lady Gregorie, that the instances of which you speak are rare. Of course, there *may* exist such cases—"

"And, in those cases, would it not be

more Christianlike," interrupted Florence hotly, "to give the suspected one the benefit of the doubt? We will not, however, continue this discussion; only," she added, with a smile which was one of her chief attractions, "I shall insist, as a penance on your venturing to disagree with me, on your reading aloud (you have a talent, I know, for recitation) a few lines from one of my favourite poets."

As she spoke, she took from a table near her a beautifully-bound volume, and having turned over a few of its leaves, she presented the book open to her companion. "You know the lines I daresay," she added, as he took it from her hand; "but they are so sweet that I can never hear them too often. Begin, please, at the words, 'Who made the heart.'"

Now it did not chance that Mr Warburton had, in the course of his studies, made himself acquainted with the works of Burns, so that when, after rising to receive the book, he glanced at the open page and saw that the verses which he was desired to read were addressed "To the Unco Guid," his pale cheek flushed, and he prepared, unwillingly enough, to perform his allotted task. He could perceive, however, no means of escape, and therefore began, with a somewhat faltering voice, to read his own condemnation :—

> " ' Who made the heart, 'tis He alone
>   Decidedly can try us,
> He knows each chord—its various tone,
>   Each spring its various bias ;
> Then at the balance let's be mute,
>   We never can adjust it ;
> What's done we partly may compute,
>   But know not what's resisted.' "

"Thanks, very much," said Lady Gregorie sweetly, when the Curate, with a heightened colour, had dreed his weird, and closed the book from which he had been slowly reading. "You have not, I see, lost your pleasant talent for recitation, and I am sorry that our approaching departure for St Margaret's will deprive us of a more frequent pleasure of taking advantage of your gift."

She shook hands with the discomfited man as she said the flattering words, and he left her gentle presence, a wiser, and it is to be hoped, a better man.

.   .   .   .

For the sorrow of Gertrude Denham, in whose lot the reader may perchance feel a passing interest, the whirligig of Time brought with it its revenge. On first, by means of the Public Press, learning that the man she loved was amongst the slain, the intelligence seemed to turn her into stone; and once again it was only the intense fear under which she laboured lest her husband should suspect the truth, which compelled her to self-command. But although one overpowering passion, namely, that of Fear, crushed down, to outward appearance, the emotions of dull despair, the effects of the shock she had received became daily more visible in the health as well as in the personal appearance of this most unhappy though guiltless woman. There was visible in her countenance the wan and weary look which is only observable in those whose hope of happiness in this life is utterly at an end; the remains of youthful beauty had faded from her face, and her days were spent in pre-

paration for the release from suffering
which could not, she felt persuaded,
be long delayed. The fulfilment of these
hopes, for hopes in truth they were,
would probably not have been for any
considerable time put off, but for an
event which, soon after the disaster in
the Soudan, changed the tenor of Gertrude Denham's life. This event was
the sudden death, in a fit of apoplexy, of
her husband. The shock to Gertrude,
whose sense of religion was strong, and
whose faith in Scripture truths was
firmly fixed as though written by a pen
of iron upon a rock, was very great.
It was terrible to believe, as believe
she did, that for the selfish profligate
who in life had denied the existence
of a God, there could, in the world
to which he had been summoned, exist

nought save a future of eternal punishment. For a woman so gentle and tender of heart as was Gertrude, the belief in such a creed as this strikes in the light of an anomaly. That the dogma was one which, from her earliest childhood, had been familiar to her, could alone account for the pertinacity with which, as an article of faith, she clung to it; and yet, whilst the shock she received was yet recent, a still small voice seemed to whisper in her ear that the God whom Christians are so frequently, in Holy Writ, enjoined to love, could not be the unjust tyrant which, in the opinion of many of His creatures, He is held to be; and it was with the faint hope of receiving comfort from his ministrations that she, on the day previous to the

funeral, requested the favour of a visit
at her house from the clergyman of
her parish. Now the Reverend Mark
Truman was an anti-Ritualist of the
most marked proclivities, and consequently the interview between him and
his bereaved parishioner led to no satis-
factory results. Mr Truman, who was
a thin, ascetic-looking man, with a cast
in his eye, and who could, "an he
would," have boasted of one of the
longest and straightest of clerical backs,
held out to her no shadow of hope
that her quondam tyrant would escape
the punishment due to his transgres-
sions. This very decided declaration of
faith produced, as I before said, a
very depressing effect upon Gertrude's
spirits ; nevertheless she, after a while,
began to realise the fact that there

was blessed peace in the house now
that the voice, which for her had been
far oftener raised in curses than in
kindness, was no longer heard within
its walls. She was, to borrow a con-
ventional term, tolerably "well left,"
for the soul of Richard Denham had
been so suddenly required of him, that
the drawing up on his part of a last
will and testament was rendered impossible. The money of which Gertrude thus became possessed was suffi-
cient not only for her own needs but
for the works of charity to which
she thenceforth intended to devote herself, and as there existed old family
ties which drew her to the pleasant
garrison town in which the Chalkshire
Rifles were for the present quartered,
she betook herself to the southern

watering-place, in which, for the remainder of her days, she hoped to sojourn.

It was by the dying bed of a woman who had been a sinner, that Gertrude Denham and the mother of the girl whom Guy Leycester had loved, first met. The widows were both clad in mourning garments, and on the countenances of each were to be read traces of recent sorrow. One marked difference, however, between the two, might by a keen observer of diagnostics have been remarked; for whereas the expression borne by the younger woman's still attractive face was that of utter despondency, there could, on her fellow-mourner's gentle features, be traced a chastened cheerfulness which at once fascinated her fellow-worker in a deed

of charity. The acquaintance thus unexpectedly commenced, soon ripened into
intimacy, for, even if Mrs Durant had
doubted the truth, which was indeed
not the case, of Guy Leycester's assurance that his relations with Mrs Denham
had not exceeded the bounds of friendship, the more she saw of Gertrude the
more thorough became her conviction
that the friend whom she had learned
to love had passed unscathed through
the fiery ordeal of temptation.

And in time, better consequences still
arose than this from the friendship which
grew up between the widows; for,
through Mrs Durant's influence and
example, Gertrude gradually abjured the
gloomy tenets in the belief in which
she had been brought up. It could
never in after days be said of her that

she was an habitually cheerful woman.
In her life there had been so little sunshine that the blossoms of early Spring
time had been too effectually nipped in
the bud for sweet flowers ever to
enliven her path again, still, amongst
the poor and the suffering, she was an
indefatigable and a glad-seeming worker;
and very thankful was she that, in the
face of apparently insurmountable difficulties, and although the tongues of
scandal had been busy with her name,
good women, and notably amongst
these were Helen Elphinstone and Lady
Gregorie, did not withhold from her
the right hand of friendship. It was
pleasant to be cared for by those to
whom Guy Leycester had been dear;
but there were times and seasons when,
in her lonely cottage by the sea, the

memory of many an early sorrow would wring her heart with unavailing grief. Times, too, there were, when the image of the dead hero whose remains lay mouldering in the arid sands of the Soudan, would rise up before her, and fill her eyes with tears; and on those occasions, when "the burden that was laid upon her seemed greater than she could bear," her thoughts would involuntarily return to some old lines which long ago, and in a half-forgotten volume, she had read :—

" Had some good Angel op'd the book of Providence,
        And let me read my Fate ;
My heart had broke when I beheld the sum of ills
        Which one by one I have endured."

CHAPTER VII.

ON THE BATTLE-FIELD.

EVER since the affair of the diamond robbery, Sir Wilfred Gregorie had been an altered man. If it be true—as true it doubtless is—that "to be wroth with those we love doth work like madness in the brain," it is equally certain that a condition of uncertainty, one which scarcely permits of any mental outbreak, but which nevertheless is a haunting evil, acts as a perpetual blister on the nerves. The Colonel was not angry, as

the saying is, with his wife, neither did
he suspect her of any act which could
be considered worse than folly, but the
consciousness that a cloud had come between him and his once entirely-trusted
Florence, was ever present with him. At
the beginning, it had seemed no bigger
than a man's hand, but the little rift
had, by slow and imperceptible degrees,
become wider, and " the pitied speck
upon the garnered fruit " had spread.

Under these circumstances, it is not
surprising that Sir Wilfred's temper,
which had never been his strong point,
should have been slightly influenced by
the present almost sunless atmosphere
of his home, and that he should have
shown signs, if not, as Captain Elphinstone had hinted, of a " martinet " like
tendency, but that he should have grown

"fussy" and difficult to please. He had become cognisant of the fact that Brereton's possession of the missing diamonds had been noised abroad, and the terrible idea that comments affecting his wife might, in consequence of his refusal to prosecute, have been made, did not tend to the improvement of his temper. Although his nature was, as a rule, little prone to "pry into abuses," the fact that the letters, which, as he had been assured, contained nothing more reprehensible than words of childish folly, had been so immediately destroyed, was constantly, and that in no agreeable fashion, recurring to his mind; and thus it unfortunately fell about that, in spite of his wife's efforts to give him pleasure, better times had not as yet begun to dawn for the now often dejected partner of the Colonel's life. That clear-sighted individual had, as I have before said, placed unlimited faith in his wife's purity of thought and action, but the pride and reserve which formed the salient points of his thoroughly manly character, were sorely wounded whenever the idea crossed his mind (and the occurrence was not a rare one), that his wife and the " unmitigated snob " who so richly deserved a horse-whipping, had had at more than one period of their mutual lives, a secret in common ; and it was this reflection which lent a coldness to his manner towards his wife, from which she deeply, although uncomplainingly, suffered.

"He will never be the same to me again," she moaned to herself; and indeed, when weeks passed away, and

she still missed the loving words and
much - prized caresses of her autocrat,
there seemed good reason to fear that
the cold austerity of the Colonel's demeanour towards his wife might become a chronic and enduring evil. Often
and bitterly did Florence lament her
folly in that she had wantonly destroyed the harmless letters which would,
she believed, have carried conviction of
her truthfulness to her husband's mind ;
but regrets were, she told herself, but
vain and profitless things, and she
therefore could only trust to Time, and
to her own unfailing gentleness and
patience, for the recovery of the loving
confidence which, in her cowardly folly,
she had thrown away.

Something she hoped from the change,
which was now near at hand, of

the quarters of the Rifles. Everything at Broadmere must, Florence told herself, remind her husband of the worries which he had gone through. But at St Margaret's all would be different. That horrid Major Brereton would be forgotten, and the cloud which the sorrows and the miseries of the last few months had thrown over her once happy life would pass away as a dream that is told. These hopes, however, did not seem, for the present at least, likely to be realised. In her new home on the South Parade, a home which flowers and sunshine, together with every luxury that wealth could procure for her delectation, were given her to enjoy, the "skeleton" still grinned ghastily from its cupboard, and "things," in the Colonel's household, were far from being "what they seemed."

To outward appearance, there was no sign or symptom of the existence, in that well-conducted household, of a familiar spirit, which, odious and uninvited, sat at the Colonel's board, and, as "the canker galls the infants of the Spring," nipped in the bud each dawning hope of better things to come.

It was in their joint ownership in little Freddie that, during that darkened period of her life, Florence trusted most that a more sunny future might eventually open out before her. There came, however, a moment when even this pillar of hope was rudely shaken, and when the joyous shout of the happy child sounded no longer in her ears, as the harbinger of future happiness. It was soon after their arrival at St Margaret's, and before the final arrange-

ments for the comfort of the occu-
pants of the new home had been com-
pleted, that the edifice to which she had
so confidently clung, began to crumble
away.

On one especial morning it happened
that, owing to the dilatoriness of the
workmen who were engaged in paper-
ing the Colonel's study, he had found
it necessary to write his letters, and get
through sundry other head work in the
dining-room. The breakfast service had
been cleared away, and Florence had
given orders that Sir Wilfred was not
to be disturbed, when over-indulged
Freddie, escaping from his nurse's control, made a noisy inroad into the
room. He was in all the glory of his
first sailor's suit, and, whip in hand,
was, in exuberant spirits, anticipating the

delight of his first ride, since Donald, the Shetland pony, had arrived from Broadmere. With the happy freedom from fear of consequences which is the lot, until he is old enough to become a nuisance, of an only and over-indulged boy, Freddie, oblivious of the respect which is a father's rightful due, suddenly, and without warning given, sprang from " behind backs " upon his parent's shoulders, and commenced taking playful liberties with his ears. Unfortunately, the time for indulgence in that species of light-hearted onslaught was ill-chosen ; the Colonel's attention was fully occupied by knotty military business, and therefore there may be some excuse for the oath, not a very bitter one, after all, which, in a moment of irritation, he launched at the innocent head of his heir-apparent. Un-

happily Florence, who at the news of
her son's *escapade* had hurried to the
room, caught the anathema as it flew
from her husband's lips, and the sting
of it pierced her to the heart. With a
cry like that of some hunted animal,
she seized the bewildered little fellow
in her arms, and having deposited him
in the safe custody of old Wylie, the
stud-groom, she fled to her own room,
and there indulged in the bitterest tears
that had ever fallen from her eyes.

"If he had any love remaining for
me," she moaned, "he could not have
been so furious. My poor little darling!
Thank God, the child is too young to
understand the meaning of those awful
words, 'Confound you!' But to shout
at the poor little fellow so that the
servants could hear that he no longer

cared for either his wife or child, was too cruel,—too humiliating, and I can never—no never whilst I live," she repeated to herself, as, with her small teeth clenched, she walked to and fro the room, "feel the same for him again."

After this occurrence, the relations between the husband and wife became still more what, in newspaper language, is called "strained." Florence could not forgive the insulting words, as she mentally termed them, which had been, in a moment of irritation, hurled at her darling. She had, in fact, by dint of long dwelling upon melancholy convictions regarding her future, grown morbid in her views of existing things. Absorbed with one idea, and that a lugubrious one, she hugged to her memory the provocation of an unintentional slight, and, in consequence of this tenacity on her part, the conviction that her husband had totally ceased to love her, took absolute possession of the unhappy woman's mind. It followed, in this unfortunate state of things, that the once gay spirits and the pleasant smiles, in the absence of which even a woman so pretty as was Florence runs the risk of losing her popularity, no longer enlivened Sir Wilfred Gregorie's home, and thence it chanced that the sight of her gloomy countenance caused that gallant soldier's sense of personal injury to increase day by day in magnitude and bitterness.

.   .   .   .

The change of quarters from Broadmere to St Margaret's wrought little if

any improvement in the domestic relations of the Colonel and his wife : it happened, however, that soon after their in-
stallation in the South Parade " mansion "
which had been made ready for their
reception, an event occurred which, affecting as it did the wellbeing of the
Chalkshire Rifles at large, did more
particularly concern that of Sir Wilfred
Gregorie's wife. The event was no
other than the bestowal on Dr Brathwaite
the highly-valued surgeon of the regiment, of a Staff medical appointment in
Ireland. Great and universal was the
regret felt by the corps at his removal
from amongst them ; and when it was
announced that his successor was, comparatively speaking, *quite* a young man,
the wives of the regiment shook their
heads, and foretold amongst themselves

not a few of the evils which, when a
doctor is unmarried and under forty, were
safe, in their opinion, to ensue.

By Lady Gregorie, who, since the commencement of her domestic troubles, had
developed a tendency to nervousness, and
to causeless fears to which she had
hitherto been a stranger, the departure
of the clever kindly doctor to whom,
as a "family man," she could, without reserve, open out the budget (not
alone of her real, but of her imaginary
troubles), was sorely lamented over. Never
again, she declared, could another doctor
take the place which Surgeon Brathwaite,
rough as was his exterior, and plain
though he was in speech, had occupied
in her esteem. It was in vain she heard
that Edgar Cranston, the young man
who had been appointed to succeed him,

was in every way worthy of the post; her objections (they being the result of foolish foregone conclusions) were not, by force of reasoning, to be overcome, and it was therefore left to the new-comer to work his way, if such a thing were feasible, into her good graces.

The newly-appointed *medico* was the fourth son of a poor Scotch baronet, and, in that he had not yet attained his thirty-second year, there was some ex-cuse for the accusation of over-youthful-ness which had been brought against him. But although young in years, he was old in experience; he had worked hard and successfully in the profession he had chosen, and, three years pre-viously, his father's interest at the Horse Guards had obtained for him the ap-pointment of Surgeon to a regiment which was on active service in Egypt. At the moment of the terrible "surprise," and during the consequent massacre in the zareba, he had taken both an active and an heroic part. Although belonging to a non-fighting branch of the service, he had, when every strong right arm was needed for that Army's rescue, fought a brave hand-to-hand battle with the desperate fanatics who, naked and utterly fearless, swarmed in their thousands to the attack. It was during the fiercest of the fray that a Marine, lying wounded and helpless on the ground, would infallibly have "lost the number of his mess," had not Surgeon Cranston, planting himself suddenly across the soldier's body, received through the fleshy part of his left arm the thrust of an Arab's spear. With the

right he fired the last shot in his revolver
at the naked breast of the assailant, and
then was just in time to catch, as it
fell heavily to earth, the falling body
of an officer, Guy Leycester by name,
who had but a short time previously
joined the regiment in which he (Edgar
Cranston) served.

In the thickest of that dreadful battle-
field, where the fight raged hottest, and
the red blood of friend and foe co-
mingled, ran in a continuous stream, there
might the tall form of Guy Leycester be
seen making effectual head against the
countless numbers by which the little
army of martyrs was being assailed.
But, as the reader has already learnt, he
fell at last! Fell, just as the Square, which
he had so well aided to re-form, stood
firm, as British infantry Squares alone can

stand ; and within that impregnable for-
tress one of England's bravest soldiers
yielded up his breath.

By the magnificent form of one of the
finest men in the British army knelt
Edgar Cranston, and as he watched with
tearful eyes the last faint struggles of
the dying man for breath, the Surgeon,
although he mentally acknowledged the
truth of the philosopher's axiom, that
" whilst War slays its thousands, Peace
does to death its tens of thousands,"
could nevertheless have cursed the mad
ambitions of the few which on the
many brings such fearful suffering and
slaughter.

For the brave work he did that day,
Edgar Cranston was rewarded by the
decoration of the Victoria Cross ; but it
was through little short of a miracle that

he lived to be gratified by its possession. His wound, neglected at first, assumed, in the uncongenial climate of Southern Africa, a serious aspect; then fever supervened, and his only chance of life lay in his removal to the floating hospital in which, during several weeks, he lay unconscious. At length, weak and helpless as a child, he was invalided home, a home which, at one time, he had never hoped to see again. Youth, however, and an excellent constitution, being in his favour, he, sooner by far than could have been expected, recovered both his health and spirits. His exchange into the Chalkshire Rifles, an object on which his mind was set, followed soon after, and it need hardly be said that by Guy Leycester's former comrades, the man who, as he lay a-dying, had ministered to their hero, was received with open arms.

Without being, strictly speaking, handsome, Edgar Cranston, with his blue eyes, auburn hair, and cheerful, kindly expression of countenance, was in the habit of meeting, from the dangerous sex, quite as much admiration as was good for him; but he was not conceited, and, moreover, he saw, soon after he joined the Rifles, one who, from the moment when his eyes beheld her, became his ideal, his safeguard, and the lady, albeit, she guessed it not, of his love.

CHAPTER VIII.

ONLY A DOCTOR.

THIS unpretending story of mine is enriched, as my readers may possibly have noticed, with the presence of three heroines at the very least. The number is, I confess, an unusual one, and, moreover, I have to tender my apologies in that no single one of that number can put forward the slightest claim to strong-mindedness. No shred even from the mantle of a Becky Sharp has fallen upon any one of them, they must therefore trust almost entirely to their virtues and their misfortunes for any passing interest which they may have been able to inspire.

When last we caught a glimpse of poor little May Durant, she was watching, from her sunny window which had a view on the St Margaret's Parade, the gaily-dressed and happy-looking girls who, escorted by one or more members of the male sex (soldiers in uniform for the most part), were taking sauntering "constitutionals" to and fro the crowded promenade. She was very young, poor child, and may surely be forgiven if a great longing to be also happy surged up, as she gazed, within her breast. In the spring time of life, a maiden's fancy will turn, and that not always lightly, to thoughts of love ; nor

do those thoughts occur less often, and
with less intensity, when the said maiden
has already known the joy of loving and
being beloved ; on the contrary, the longing for the

> "Touch of a vanished hand,
> And the sound of a voice that is still,"

is not unfrequently the forerunner of
dreams, unbidden and often sorely
regretted, of another being, different,
it may be, as possible from the first
love of her heart, but whose image
will persist, even whilst she is wrapped
in slumber, in obtruding itself upon
her fancy.

Second marriages have, by some woman-
hating cynic, been characterised as "the
triumph of hope over experience," but, in
my opinion, the most frequent amongst
the causes of such ventures, is the hope

of finding again a protector and a friend. It fell once to my lot (and gladly would I have been excused the task) to break to a middle-aged widow the terrible news of her husband's unexpected death. She had been during many years the devoted wife of a sickly, asthmatical invalid, who, during a short absence of his wife's to visit a dying mother, had suddenly succumbed to a sharp attack of breathlessness. It so happened that I was the only available friend by whom the short railway journey could be performed, and the sad intelligence imparted to the widow, and therefore I, with an unwilling mind, proceeded on my mission. As the Train in which I was seated sped along, I beguiled the time by reflecting in what terms I should first address my sorrowing friend. It was impossible—that fact was very certain—to repeat to her in form of consolation the remark which the brother of the deceased, a gouty bachelor of fifty-five, had, previous to my departure, whispered in my ear, the remark, namely, that poor Ned's death was a happy release; and seeing that no more feasible plan did, in the course of a long hour and a half, occur to me, I had to trust to a chance inspiration for success in my lugubrious undertaking.

Happily for me, the length of my face, together with my unexpected presence in her mother's house, told my tale, and rendered speech unnecessary. "Oh!" exclaimed the stricken woman, "he is gone, and I was not with him," and as she spoke, the tears fell in torrents from her eyes. What were the words which I, in my poor attempts at consolation, murmured, I have, of course, forgotten, but my mental relief was great when she, a fine, buxom woman still, dried her eyes, and gave utterance between her sobs to the following, in my humble opinion, very sensible words :—"I am," she said, calmly but very sadly, "most unfortunately situated in regard to widowhood. If I were a young woman, I might in time look forward to the possibility of marrying again, or if I were old, the hope of ere long finding rest in the grave would buoy up my spirits, but I am, unhappily, a hale woman of fifty-three, with just enough money to enable me to live respectably, so what remains for me but a life of solitude and regret ?"

Paul, the Roman citizen, whose insight into the weaknesses of human nature was decidedly keen, makes mention of " three score years " as the period of life when a widow may reasonably be expected to have " put *on* the old *woman*," and have therefore become qualified to perform correctly the serious duties of life. That there are exceptions to this rule most of us will, I think, be willing to allow; notwithstanding which difference of opinion, few will, I imagine, be likely to question the wisdom of the preacher in that he enjoined his disciple Timothy to refuse the enrolment of "younger widows" in the band of holy women who were joined together for the performance of good works. The reason given against the enrolment of these youthful mourners was, as those amongst my readers who have searched the Scriptures, must be aware, that they, not having as yet outlived the follies and blamable frivolities of their sex, would probably marry again, and thus render themselves unfit for the pious labours which would be required at their hands.

"But," my readers may possibly exclaim, "whence this discussion *quoad* widows, seeing that pretty May Durant is no husbandless bride, but simply a young girl who having once fondly loved, is surely at liberty to love again?"

True, oh sagacious critic; but she has already, in her short life, gone through experiences which justify the bestowing on her "brevet rank" as a widow. And, moreover, who can deny that the maiden who finds consolation in the possession of a *second* love is not generally popular with novel readers? They are apt to require of her a constancy which they themselves, if tempted, might not have been able to practise. It is, according to these romance-reading young ladies, the duty of the affected one, even when playing with reluctance her part in society, to coldly, and with weeping eyes, turn from the gaze of surrounding lovers, for her heart is, or, at least ought to be,

"In the land where her young hero sleeps."

Amongst those novel readers and others by whom this opinion is held, may be reckoned first and foremost little May herself. To describe with any degree of truthfulness the amount of self-disgust, nay, even of loathing, which she underwent when first the idea that she *might* possibly love again occurred to her, would be impossible; and the existence of this feeling on her

part was by her family so fully recognised that they abstained from any
premature attempts to draw her from
the atmosphere of gloom in which it
pleased her to envelop herself. By
slow degrees, however, a change was
effected, and great was Mrs Durant's
joy, when May, on her return one
morning from a quiet walk up the
Castle Hill, looked more like herself
than she had done for months. She
had met, and been introduced by her
sister to Edgar Cranston!

Now it cannot be denied that the
girl's thoughts had of late often turned
towards the man whose presence by
Guy Leycester's bed of death had given
him, Cranston, an interest in her mind
and thoughts superior to that which,
as she believed, she could ever feel

for mortal man again. On that blood-stained battle-field, where countless hordes of Arabs were mingled in wild confusion with British soldiers fighting hand to hand and inch by inch for life and for their country's honour, Edgar Cranston knelt beside the stricken hero. His eyes were the last on which those of the dying man had rested, and amidst the terrific roar of battle the feeble moan of the parting spirit had reached his ears! There came a time, but that was yet afar off, when, questioned closely by the girl who by that noble soldier had been left behind, Cranston had allowed her to believe that the sweetly-sounding name of the girl he loved had been breathed by Guy's pallid lips.

Was it a pious fraud, or had that

ardent sympathiser really taught himself to credit the fact which he asserted? If the former, may we not venture to hope that the sternest sticklers for truth at any price will, for the sake of the excellence of the motive, mercifully condone the sin.

.   .   .   .

It was not until many months had, after May's introduction to Edgar Cranston, ran their course, that the following conversation between Mrs Durant and her daugther Helen took place. The countenances of both ladies were, if not precisely anxious, nevertheless laden with an expression which foretokened a somewhat momentous disquisition. They were seated in Mrs Elphinstone's luxuriously fitted-up morning-room, the perfume of rare flowers filled the air, whilst from below, a sweet, fresh voice, the voice of May Durant, as she sang with exquisite pathos Ruth's tender appeal to Naomi, sounded faintly on the ear.

"Dear child! How glad I am that at last she can sing to us again! They are only sad songs as yet, but let us hope that the time may come when more cheerful sounds will break from her lips."

"Yes," rejoined Helen, after a short pause, and speaking as it were, under protest, "it is sweet to hear her dear voice again; but, mother darling, we must not, anxious as we of course are that May should recover her spirits, shut our eyes to the real facts of the case. Mr Cranston is in love with the dear child, and that she should in time return his affection, seems a terribly likely thing."

Mrs Durant, albeit by nature one of the simplest-minded and least suspicious of human beings, was more sorry than surprised by her daughter's exordium. She had seen enough of human nature to be aware that, even as "circumstances alter cases," so do the proclivities of human beings become modified, and that not always for the better, by any organic change in their condition. She was, in short, too wise a woman to expect perfection. "The faultless monster that the world ne'er saw," was a *lusus naturæ* in which she put no faith, and therefore it was that, whilst still recognising in her daughter Helen the virtues of personal humility and absence of ambition, she was not

unprepared for tokens, on Mrs Elphinstone's part, of opposition to Edgar
Cranston's possible suit.

Notwithstanding the *prestige* which the
latter, from various causes, enjoyed, it
could not be denied that his position in
life was, in the opinion of the worldly-
minded, inferior to that which Helen herself occupied. Her elevation to wealth
and social rank had to a certain extent
told on the character of Mrs Elphinstone.
She was ambitious for her sister, and
possibly foresaw in that sister's union
with Mr Cranston a certain loss of
"caste" for herself. She desired with all
her heart that May might once more
—as became her age and temperament—
be happy, but, having herself learned
to thoroughly enjoy the blessings
which wealth can bestow, she did

not figure to herself the possibility of her young sister being able to exist in comfort on the comparatively slender income of which an assistant regimental surgeon was probably the recipient.

Mrs Durant, although her views on the question differed from those which Helen not altogether secretly entertained, had, from the moment that Mr Cranston's attentions became marked, resolved to remain neutral; her regard, however, for the young army doctor was too sincere, and her desire for May's happiness too fervent, for the golden virtue of silence to be practicable for her now, and she therefore said, laying aside her needlework as she did so — a proof, in Mrs Elphinstone's opinion that on this occasion her dear mother intended *business*,—

"Dear Nellie, I have not, any more than have you, shut my eyes to what may, in consequence of Mr Cranston's attentions, follow for our darling, but I cannot agree with you in thinking that, could she be brought to love him, the result would be for her an unfortunate one."

"Of course, if she really loved him, that would alter the case," Helen, after a short period given to reflection, replied; "but, dear mother, surely she cannot care for him! Think of the difference! Compare him with poor Guy — so handsome, so distinguished-look-ing—"

"Yes," sighed Mrs Durant, "he was all that, and in those respects Edgar

Cranston cannot vie with our poor friend; but do you reckon the winning of the Victoria Cross as nothing; and, moreover, although he may be less tall, I daresay, by a few inches than was Captain Leycester, his air and manners are those of a well-bred gentleman, and his features and expression—"

"Are good as good can be—I grant all that," interrupted Helen; "yet there remains the fact that he is only a doctor, and only a doctor is not good enough for May."

Mrs Durant was silent for a few moments, and then slowly repeated her daughter's words, "'Only a doctor.' Then, my Nellie," continued the agitated woman, "am I to believe that the gifts of high principle, of a sense of honour so keen that he would shrink from debt as from an act of fraud, are as nothing in your sight ? Have you overlooked his gentleness, his patience, with that most tiresome of women, his mother, and the example of self - sacrifice which, were he to die, he would, in his care of Lady Cranston, leave behind him ?"

"Say no more, mother," said Helen penitently. "You are right, and I was wrong in suggesting a comparison between Mr Cranston and poor Guy. He, the dear friend who has passed away, must, in] many respects, fatally lose by being placed side by side with your favourite ; and indeed, when I look at Mrs Denham's still beautiful face, so sad yet so resigned, I can understand the terrible mischief which such a man as Guy (a man in whose nature good and evil were so strangely mingled)

can, in his generation, do, I cannot but admit that the happiness of
any woman who had thrown in her
lot with his would rest on a very
weak foundation indeed."

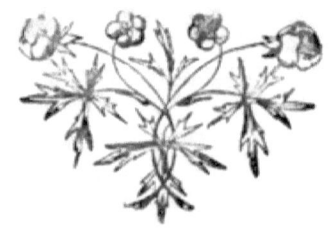

CHAPTER IX.

OLD AS THE HILLS.

IT was impossible for any lover to be more fully alive than was Edgar Cranston to the difficulties that stood in the way of his success. It was no being of mortal mould whose influence he had to combat, —no rival who might by some happy chance fall from the lofty pedestal on which the fancy of his ladye had placed him, had he, in this struggle, to contend with, for the man whose image was stamped upon her heart lay in his grave, and the dead can do no wrong.

When first the young surgeon became aware that he loved, with his whole heart and soul, the child-bride of Guy Leycester, whose death had left her mourning, his consternation was as great as was the self-abhorrence of May when she discovered that in her heart of hearts she was false to the memory of her first love. She was so far—Edgar felt— above him! Not in rank, or wealth, or social position, for was not he, alike by birth, by education, and by profession—a gentleman? And what more, or what greater thing, could he be? But the girl whom he ventured to adore was, in his imagination, a far higher thing than this. She was, in his eyes, en- nobled, nay, even sanctified, by the waters of affliction which had gone over her soul and purified it from earthly dross.

May's beauty was precisely of the kind that assimilated with the idea taken by Edgar Cranston of her temperament and proclivities. "Divinely fair" was she, with deep grey eyes shaded by dark lashes, and abundant hair of a pale golden hue, whilst so fragile of form was she that, but for the fact that she rarely suffered in health, the exceeding delicacy of her appearance could hardly have failed to awaken anxiety in the breasts of those who loved her. The style of loveliness which had fallen to May Durant's share was precisely the kind which, whilst it suited the fastidiousness of taste that was inherent in Cranston, rather encouraged than was antagonistic to the timid fashion of his wooing. May, in her white garments, with just a touch here and there of sombre black, looked, in her lover's eyes, so purely and exquisitely ethereal, that even to touch the hem of her garment struck him as an act, well nigh, of sacrilege.

In the eyes of lookers-on, no change whatever did, in the course of several months, take place in the relations between May Durant and the man who worshipped her. Time, however, "irresistible" and never idle Time, was meanwhile doing his slow but certain work. When in two young hearts (hearts, be it understood, for whom opportunities for analysing each other's feelings are neither few nor far between) Love has found an entrance, the moment when the over-full cup will brim over, and when from the passion-filled breast the lips will speak, cannot be far away.

From sundry signs and tokens, signs which probably only by a lover's watchful eye could have been perceived, Edgar Cranston had began to gather hope that the thoughts of the beloved one were not now so wholly engrossed by her dead lover as had hitherto seemed the case. On one occasion, when he, having called on Mrs Elphinstone, had chanced to find Miss Durant alone,. the latter had, on his entrance, blushed so suddenly and vividly that for a few moments an "awkward" silence reigned between the two. Nor had this been all, for when, on taking leave, he had, for the first time, ventured on the slightest pressure of her hand, he had fancied (could it be only fancy, and was Hope telling him one of those fond and flattering tales by which lovers are so often perilously beguiled?) that the half-suggestive lingering of his hand in hers had not been utterly without response.

It was about a week after this important occurrence, for important in the lovers' eyes it was, that an event occurred which, although tragical in itself, had the effect of hurrying on a *dénouement* of which some amongst May's best wishers had begun to despair. A private belonging to the Chalkshire Rifles had, in a fit, it was supposed, of mad drunkenness, fired one night at his sergeant, and shot him dead. The victim was a married man, and the father of five children. He bore an excellent character, and the despair of his young wife was so great that fears for her reason

were at the first entertained by the
military doctors by whom she was at-
tended. As may be supposed, the sympathy and compassion which her case
elicited were very great, and everything
which might tend to alleviate her grief
was by the officers of the regiment and
their wives lavishly offered to the widow.

Now May Durant and the unhappy
woman whose life had been thus suddenly rendered desolate, chanced to be
old acquaintances. Captain Elphinstone's
pretty sister-in-law loved little children
dearly, and one of Sergeant Godfrey's
flock, a chubby small girl of three, had
been taken by the young lady under
her especial protection. It had so happened that Bessie, who was rather a
spoilt child, had, on an occasion when
she was suffering from a rather severe

attack of measles, obstinately refused to swallow the medicine which had been prescribed for her.

"Oh, Miss May, whatever shall we do?" the anxious mother exclaimed, when Miss Durant, having heard of the child's illness, had called to inquire after her little friend. "Here's Bessie that naughty she won't open her mouth to take the doctor's physic, and he says as the measles may take a bad turn if the fever aint kep' down."

"But the naughty fever will be kept down," May, seating herself by the bedside, and speaking in her soft, coaxing way, whispered to the refractory patient. "Bessie and I will keep him down between us. Bessie is going to be a brave girl, and if she fights a good fight, why, we shall see to-morrow

what reward she will have. But first,"
she added, as the patient raised her
head from the pillow, and displayed
signs of returning sense, "let me see
if this stuff is so very nasty after all;"
and so saying, May, having put her
rosy lips to the medicine cup, continued
her attempts at persuasion.

To that task, one which happily
proved successful, we will leave her,
and return to the heart-stricken woman,
who, surrounded by her orphan children,
could, in the first shock of her bereavement, see in their possession less than
no sources of consolation. It is winter
time, and she is seated by a fire which,
through neglect, has burned low in the
hearth, a cup of untasted tea is on the
small deal table beside her chair, and
the little ones, of whom three-year-

old Bessie is the third in age, are standing about in various abnormal attitudes, and with countenances in which wonder and curiosity are plainly visible. By the poor widow's side, and holding her toil-hardened hand closely pressed within her own, sits May Durant. She has been listening, during a slowly-passing hour, with a tender patience that is born of her own experience in sorrow, to Mrs Godfrey's tautological wailings over her loss. The stereotyped arguments to which those who attempt to reason away despair are driven to resort, had proved, soft and sympathising as had been the words and intonation of the speaker, utterly unavailing; the widow, like Rachel of old, refused to be comforted, and May, after repeating for the twentieth time

the comforting assurance that the fact
of Sergeant Godfrey having been so
exemplary a husband and father would
ensure for him and the mother of his
children a happy meeting in the world
beyond the grave, was about to make
preparations for her departure, when
the door opened noiselessly, and Edgar
Cranston, with an almost silent footfall,
entered the dimly-lighted room.

The short winter twilight had already
began to overshadow the scene, and,
as I have already said, the fire in the
little room was beginning to burn low, so
that it was only by a lover's instinct
that Cranston recognised the tall figure,
which on his entrance rose to meet him,
as that of May Durant. He took her
offered hand in silence, and then, without addressing her, spoke in pleasant-

sounding words to the bereaved one. And she— Well! she, poor soul, under the influence of his very presence, brightened up in a manner that, to May, whose efforts at consolation had been so unavailing, seemed to border on the miraculous. Truly it is good, when the voice of a man is gentle as well as firm, to listen to its accents! There is, to feeble women, encouragement to suffer bravely, in the mere propinquity of one stronger, both physically and mentally, than themselves, and thus it was that when Edgar Cranston spoke to the Sergeant's widow of her husband's courage in battle, of the medals that he had won, and of the certainty that the children of so good a soldier would not, by a grateful country, be forgotten, the mourner's sobs were hushed, and the

future of her life looked less utterly
dark and dreary.

And for May Durant the spell of the
soldier-surgeon's presence worked scarcely
less powerfully. In the semi-obscurity,
the slight and militarily erect figure, clad
in the dark green uniform of his regiment, brought to her mind with such
strange vividness the form of the lover
she had lost, that for a few moments
she stood motionless, whilst a constriction
in her throat—the *globus hystericus* to
which sensitive natures are subject—
caused her to feel infinitely relieved in
that she was for the nonce not called
upon to speak. In silence she listened
to the brave words in which the man
who had supported in death the dear
head of her soldier-lover, brought comfort to the widow's heart; but when,

after a short pause, he turned towards
her, and, in a pleasant, unemotional
voice, said,—"Is it not rather late, Miss
Durant, for you to be so far from
home?" the power to reply absolutely
failed her, and a sensation of faintness,
the result partly of nervous tremor,
caused her to fall back upon the chair
from which she had risen.

At that moment, a sudden light,
the result of some matches which the
widow's eldest hope had thrown upon
the well-nigh expiring embers, revealed
to Cranston the fact of May's deathlike
pallor.

"Good God!" he exclaimed, "you are
ill—fainting. It is the closeness of the
room;" and opening wide the window
near which she was seated, he, with
fingers which were none of the steadiest,

unfastened her sealskin jacket, and allowed the fresh air to play over her face and throat; then when she began to recover, he said gently, but in a voice which quavered slightly,—

"You are over-exerting yourself. Let me take you into the air," and, encircling her waist with his arm, he drew her towards the open door.

She made no attempt to withdraw herself from his supporting arm, but, after one or two long-drawn breaths, murmured a few broken sentences.

"My sister was to send the carriage. Is it very late? I feel so weak—" and then, letting her fair head lean against his shoulder, a flood of tears came to her relief.

He was only human, that poor young doctor who had worshipped so long his idol from afar. She had been to him only as an angel until then; but now — now when she lay restfully in his embrace, when the close contact with her exquisite form filled his veins with the fire of a man's fierce passion, is it surprising that he should have lost his head? For lose it he did— temporarily at least, but in no mild measure; for the kiss which he in his ecstatic madness pressed upon May's ripe lips, was no timid caress, — no hastily-stolen pleasure, but the long, deep draught of a thirsty man who, having performed a long journey through an arid wilderness, cannot bring himself to take from his lips the cup which is to him as nectar.

And May, what, during that moment when the flood-gates of her lover's passion were opened, was her young heart saying? Was it fear of the growing obscurity, or dread of a return of the strange faintness from which she was recovering, that caused her to remain a willing prisoner in the strong arms of her sweetheart?

To these queries we must — modest young maiden although May doubtless was — answer in the negative; for the spell that held her there was, albeit she knew it not, also of Passion's weaving, and—

> " The languor of a soul too richly blest
> Kept her a willing captive in her lover's clasp."

I will not attempt to excuse her. The night was closing in, and, for they had walked slowly down the hill on which the barracks are situated, she is virtually alone with a man who has just ventured on as outrageous a liberty as can well be taken by a wooer; but what will you? as the French, in their smoother-sounding language, say. For months the poor child had, unsuspected in its full intensity by herself, been pining for a love which would call back to her the days when Passion's language spoke to her in every look of Guy's, and when kisses, fond as his, would awake her from the cold reality of her daily life.

And now, as Edgar Cranston, half-remorseful, but with the blissful memory of that stolen kiss still present with him, and with May's little hand held closely within his arm, has found words wherewith to tell his tale, she listens as though entranced.

"Have I been too bold, sweet May?" he said. "If so, you must forgive me. It is so long since I began to love you, and when a hope, slight as it was, sprang up in my heart that you might learn to care for me, the joy was too much, and I, being but a weak and erring mortal, yielded to temptation."

"It was my fault," she murmured. "I was frightened; and you have been always good to me."

"Good to you, my angel! Ah, my love, my darling, who would not be good to one so pure and gentle? Say, will you trust your life's happiness in my hands? Do you think that you can learn to love me?"

She did not answer him in words, but the pressure of her gentle fingers on his arm told him that he had not asked in vain, and the soldier-surgeon, who had won his laurels on the battle-field, but whose courage had waxed faint in the presence of the girl he loved, grew of a sudden so recklessly brave that, under cover of the darkness, and the absence of passers-by, he drew her once more within the shelter of his breast, and covered her sweet face with kisses.

CHAPTER X.

A NOBLE DEED.

"I AM so glad you have grown to think Mr Cranston nice and clever, as we do. Singleton and I quite swear by him; but I felt sure that you would be of our opinion in time."

It is Lady Adela Singleton, the recently married wife of one of the Chalkshire Captains, who, seated one sunny forenoon on a bench on the Parade, has given to her friend and present companion, Lady Gregorie, the benefit of *her* opinions regarding the Scotch doctor's merits. The Colonel's wife, whose attention is engrossed by little Freddie's unwonted pallor, and by his somewhat languid attitude as he leans against her knee, does not immediately reply, and therefore Lady Adela, whose tongue is rarely, on ordinary occasions, silent, continues her panegyric thus :—

"Singleton says that if he had ever so severe an illness, and the worst possible hunting accident, he would have no other doctor than Mr Cranston. He is so prompt, Jack says, so self-reliant. And you, I am sure you trust him, dear Lady Gregorie? You think him clever, don't you?"

"Yes; he is clever, of course, and very nice, and gentleman-like, but I was so fond of our old doctor, that I hardly think I shall ever like another quite as well."

At that moment a child's voice, that of Freddie, broke in, sharp and querulous, on the dialogue, and the little fellow, in his sailor's suit, leant more heavily than before against his mother.

"Oh, Mamsey!" the plaintive voice sobbed out, "my throat hurts me; and so does my head," and the boy, tossing aside the straw hat, on which might be read by every passer-by the grandiloquent word "Majestic," rested his sunny curls, in languid fashion, on the soft velvet of his mother's lap, and his breath came short and pantingly.

In wild alarm, Lady Gregorie would have lifted him in her arms, but her strength failed her; and then, rising quickly from the bench, she, with a supporting arm passed round the child, beckoned frantically to an elderly Bath-chair attendant, who, together with his empty vehicle, was happily within hail, to approach.

"Shall I run for Mr Cranston?" asked Lady Adela, who, perceiving that little Freddie could not, for some as yet unexplained reason, stand alone, rightly concluded that he must be ill; "I saw his trap just now at Mrs Winters' door;" and the energetic young woman, without waiting to be thanked, hurried off at once on her important quest.

With the assistance of the elderly chairman, Florence, although shaking with nervous trepidation, contrived to settle her boy comfortably in the, to him, unaccustomed vehicle, and he, momentarily aroused by the novelty of the situation from the stupor of approaching illness, smiled wanly in his mother's bent down face, as the words, "Make the gee go faster," came brokenly from his lips.

The Colonel from his study window noted the abnormal procession, and understanding at once that something was the matter, *his* was the hand which, before the bell could be rung, flung open the house door, and *his* the arms which, lifting the now unconscious child from the chair, carried him, with the tender care that is inspired by love and fear combined, up the broad staircase to his bed. Then with a *catch* in the voice that was usually so clear and resonant, he said to the poor mother, who hung like one bereft of sense over her darling,—

" When did this happen ? Have you sent for Cranston ? "

" Yes—but he may be out; and this— this— Ah! there is no time," she gasped, " to lose — is — I feel terribly afraid — diphtheria."

At the sound of that dreaded word, Sir Wilfred, with the object of seeking in any and every direction for medical help, rushed from the room ; but on the stairs he found himself, to his great joy, face to face with Edgar Cranston.

" Well, what is the matter with the little chap ? " the latter was, in his cheery way, beginning, when, catching sight of Sir Wilfred's serious countenance, he felt instinctively that the cheerfulness which as a rule, he, in cases of mild sickness, advocated, was just now out of place.

"Come this way. We are horribly frightened," said the Colonel. "My wife thinks that it is," and the strong man shuddered inwardly as he pronounced the word, "diphtheria."

"Let us hope otherwise," said the Surgeon, in a low voice, as he followed his host to the sick child's room. "It is probably only a slight case of throat inflammation, and Lady Gregorie's alarm may, after all, be causeless."

On his entrance, Florence sprang from the bedside towards him, and, laying her hand on his arm, entreated him, in passionate accents, to cure her boy. "He will die," she cried, "if you do not save him, and he is all I have." Then the Colonel's stern voice spoke out.

"Compose yourself, Florence," he said, "and instead of this wild raving, allow Mr Cranston to see what ails the child. Sit down, and try not to be a fool."

He did not mean to be unkind, but he felt the necessity of checking the hysterical display of his wife's feelings; and then a man who is striving his utmost to control his own strong emotions, may be forgiven the passing outburst of impatience which a woman's exhibition of weakness causes him to experience. After this crushing, but doubtless salutary, rebuke, poor Florence subsided into agonising silence. Her cup was indeed full now to overflowing, the relief even of tears was denied to her; by what perhaps the dying bed of her child his father could have the heart to speak harshly to her, and now her only wish was to lie down by Freddie's side, in the rest and quiet of the grave.

Meanwhile Edgar Cranston was, with a grave face, and concentrated attention, examining the diagnostics of his patient's malady. How anxiously they watched him, those two, whose only child, a frail blossom of but a few years old, was fighting a hard battle for existence with the reaper Death! And when he, the man on whose fiat the hopes and fears of those poor parents were hanging, raised himself from his stooping posture, and in a quiet tone asked Lady Gregorie a common-place question, part of the weight upon their hearts seemed taken off, for not as yet were they to hear the sentence which it might be the doctor's painful duty to pronounce.

"When did the child first complain of his throat?" he inquired.

"Yesterday," faltered Florence; "but I gave him one of Dr Brathwaite's little powders, and in the evening he seemed better. He could breathe quite freely then, and I never thought that—"

"There was anything serious the matter. I quite understand. These cases always come on suddenly. There may, possibly—do not be alarmed, for I only speak of a problematical event— arise the necessity for a slight opera- tion, and, in that case, I should be glad, if you have no objection, to ask either Mr Gilchrist or Dr Fendall to be present."

"Certainly, certainly," replied Sir Wil- fred, whose alarm, at the mere mention of an operation, had increased tenfold, and he was preparing to give the necessary orders for the attendance in hot haste of additional medical aid, when the face of the little sufferer, who, with the exception of his somewhat laboured respiration, had not hitherto exhibited any of the worst and most fatal symptoms of his awful malady, suddenly became almost of a purple hue, and the struggle for breath, and consequently for life, was fearful to witness. For this terrible emergency, the army surgeon was happily not unprepared. Several cases of diphtheria had recently appeared in the town, and two of Dr Gilchrist's patients had fallen victims to a disease which seldom spares those on whom it has fixed its fangs. Edgar Cranston had hitherto been more fortunate, but, knowing, as full well he did, that there is often a crisis in the malady, when the performance of a dangerous operation can alone give the sufferer a chance for life, such contingencies as the present did not find him wanting. In a moment his surgical case was opened, and, choosing a sharp *bistoury*, he, with a steady and un-shrinking hand, skilfully plunged it into the trachea. In a moment the breathing was relieved, the risk of suffocation dis-appeared, and danger was, for the present, warded off.

His next move, one which he per-forms with surprising celerity, is to insert into the wound a silver tube through which the respiration of the little fellow who is being thus snatched from death comes softly as that of an unweaned child, and the mother, on her knees beside the bed (in the coverlet of which she has, during the operation, hidden her face), offers up a fervent thanksgiving to God for the great mercy which has been vouchsafed to her.

But, alas! all is not yet over, for scarcely has Sir Wilfred ceased from expressing to the operator his gratitude and joy, and whilst that operator himself is still feeling, although his outward calm is undisturbed, somewhat unhinged by the demand which had been suddenly made upon his skill and self-command, a farther and more trying call is made upon his courage. Whilst looking about, preparatory to taking his departure, for his hat, he is painfully struck by a change which in his little patient he perceives; once more the child is struggling for breath, and symptoms of suffocation are again imminent. Not for a second does Edgar hesitate, either as regards the cause of this unexpected relapse, or as to the only course, which, in order to save that precious life, remains to be taken. Being well acquainted with every phase and characteristic of the dangerous complaint which he has been called upon to combat, Cranston immediately realises the circumstance that a piece of false membrane (no uncommon case) has made its way into the tube, and blocked it up! For this evil there exists but one remedy, a desperate one, as the young surgeon, with his professional acumen, fully realises, and that remedy consists in the sucking from the tube, by a stander-by, the substance which has lodged in it. The chances are, as he is thoroughly aware, a thousand to one against the survival of the individual by whom this truly heroic act of self-sacrifice has been performed, and he may, perhaps, be forgiven if the thought flashes across his mind that *perhaps* the father of this idiolised child *may* take upon himself the perilous duty, from which weak human nature shrinks appalled. The notion, however, lasts but a moment; Sir Wilfred is both too ignorant and too paralysed by alarm to interfere, and so, with a glance full of tender pity at the kneeling mother, and another at the man, standing erect with folded arms, but with agony depicted on every feature of his death pale face, the soldier-surgeon, without a thought of self, applies his mouth to the tube, and, by the act of inhalation, draws away the obnoxious element, and thus, for the second time, by his skill and courage, saves the life of the Colonel's son.

CHAPTER XI.

L'ENVOI.

IT is early spring at St Margaret's. The sun is shining brightly, and the air is perfumed with the breath of violets and wall-flowers. The band of the Chalkshire Rifles is playing lively music on the Parade, whilst gaily-dressed girls and lively matrons are chatting, laughing, and, it may be, tell it not in Gath, flirting and spreading scandal.

On one of the benches is seated Florence Gregory, whilst by her side, and whispering quietly in response to the animated converse of the Colonel's wife, is May Durant. It is the eve of the girl's wedding-day, and although she is happy, she feels sad.

"Now, May, dear," Lady Gregorie is saying, "remember this; Edgar Cranston has not a fault in the world, and if you do anything to make him unhappy, I will never forgive you."

A low girlish laugh is May's first response to her friend's threat, then she says feelingly,—

"I trust that I do not need a warning. My chief object will be to please him, and my best hope is that I may succeed."

"But you must not be disappointed, dear, if you do not; for men, even the very best, are sometimes difficult to, what is called, 'get on with;'" and Lady Gregorie sighed as she remembered how many months had passed since she had striven, and altogether, she felt, in vain, to win back her husband's love and trust.

In the terribly trying days during the slow passing of which little Freddie fought his way back to vigorous life, and also whilst to anxious watchers by his side it seemed as though only by a miracle the man who had hazarded his own existence to save their child could escape the consequences of his noble deed, the mutual anxiety of the Colonel and his wife effected between them a certain amount of *rapprochement.* Most of the time which Florence could spare from attendance on her boy was passed by her in Edgar Cranston's room; the room from which, laid low by a consuming fever, it seemed next to impossible that its occupant could ever issue forth alive. But, happily for the many who loved him, but more especially for the peace of mind of those for whose sake he had been willing to lay down his life, that life was not, as yet, at least, required of him. Youth, together with a constitution which had never been unduly tried, at length carried him through, and it is needless to add that from thenceforth he had no truer and more devoted friends than those who were powerless, strong as was their will, to repay in full the debt of gratitude which they owed to him.

Two months have now elapsed since Edgar Cranston's convalescence has become thoroughly confirmed, and the state of things between Sir Wilfred and

Lady Gregorie have returned to very much their normal groove. Freddie is once more the "pictur," as his nurse boasts, of health, and his mother's nerves are often now severely tried by the sight of her treasure caracoling on his Shetland pony by the side of her husband's charger. Sir Wilfred laughs at her fears, and at her entreaties that he will at least employ a leading-rein, in order to lessen the danger for her darling. He will not have the child made a molly-coddle of, he says, and Florence, more than ever convinced that his heart is closed against her, subsides into a distressful silence, which he, manlike, mistakes for sulks.

"For, alas! it is only too true that the love which he had felt for his fair wife was beginning to be undermined

by the coldness of her demeanour towards her lord, a coldness which he,
on his part, attributed to diminished
affection for himself. Could he but have
looked into the warm and tender heart
of the woman who bore his name, he
would have recognised his error, and,
let us hope, have hastened to repair it.

.   .   .   .

It is, as I have said, the eve of
May Durant's wedding-day, and Lady
Gregorie, after listening to the farewell
notes of "God save the Queen" from
the regimental band, has returned home
for the afternoon tea, at which ceremony
the Colonel occasionally, whilst smoking
his cigarette, puts in an appearance.
On the afternoon in question, he, with
an open newspaper in his hand, lounges
into the pretty morning-room, and is

at once accosted by Florence with the remark that Alfred Durant, who has returned from Canada in order to be best man to his brother-in-law elect, is, she thinks, greatly improved in appearance.

"Can't say that I see much difference!" growled the Colonel, who had neither forgotten nor forgiven the disgrace, as he, owing to strong *esprit de corps*, considered it, which the lad had formerly brought upon the regiment.

"May is delighted that you are going to give her away," continued Florence, who, for her husband appeared to be in no amiable temper, was doing her best to enliven him by her remarks.

"Is she? She is thankful for small mercies. She is a good girl, though, I believe, but marriage is such an awful lottery, that I wish I had something better to bestow upon the grand young fellow who is going to rush upon his fate to-morrow."

The words are not encouraging, and the tears, which in those days are only too easily summoned from their "briny depths," are with difficulty, by the mortified wife, suppressed; whilst the Colonel, whose momentary irritability is possibly soothed by a mild B.-and-S., and also by the excellence of the cigarette in which he is indulging, is running his eye over the columns of the French *Figaro;* whilst his wife, with her tea and toast untasted before her, is looking, with flushed cheeks, and an expression of extreme surprise upon her pretty face, fixedly on the first column of the *Morning Post.* She has, in a great measure, lost the habit of communicating her surprises to the Colonel, but on this occasion her astonishment is so great that it momentarily breaks down the barrier of reserve, and she exclaims aloud,—

"Oh, Wilfred! there is such a wonderful marriage in the papers! Major Brereton to Miss Emily Vidal. How can she have done such a thing! She *must* know what he is—a common thief—"

"'Birds of a feather flock together,'" said the Colonel quietly. "And now that your friend has so prosperously established herself in life, I can venture to give you a piece of information which, through regard for your feelings, I have hitherto withheld from you. The police, in the course of their officious investigations into that confounded diamond robbery, made the discovery that Miss Vidal had her share in the plunder. I never wish to hear the affair mentioned again, and I only tell you this, in order that you may be more careful in future as to your choice of friends."

Lady Gregorie's dismay on hearing that Em had acted in a manner so treacherous and so "low," was very great; there was, however, a sternness in Sir Wilfred's manner which entirely quelled her rising inclination to take the part of the accused. It grieved her much that he should leave her before she had called up courage to say a word in her friend's defence; nor were her regrets for her lack of moral courage lesssened, when, later in the day, she received the following laconic epistle from Major Brereton's newly-married wife :—

"MY DEAR FLO," so that unabashed young person wrote, "I have not above a moment to spare, but that moment I dedicate to your service. You may remember that when I delivered up to you your dearly-purchased letters, you rashly threw them, as you imagined, into the flames. I was, however, lucky enough to have my wits about me, and seeing that the papers had fallen rather short of the burning wood, I rescued them from the grate, before there had been done to them any more mischief than that of getting slightly scorched; and I now, in the hope that the reading of them will do you good service with your cross-grained Colonel, return the precious remains to your safe-keeping.

"You will doubtless see amongst the marriages the announcement of mine to Major Brereton ; wish me joy, there's a good child, and believe me, yours affectionately,   EMILY BRERETON."

Lady Gregorie's delight at this un-expected piece of good fortune was so intense that she overlooked the fami-liarity of the terms in which the *ci-devant* friend, whom she now more than half believed to be a robber, ventured to address her.

"Ah ! he will forgive me now," she said to herself, whilst reading the only slightly-singed notes, and realising to the full, the childishness and folly of their contents. "He will leave off

being stiff and cold to me, and I shall
be a happy woman once again!"

Never before, even in her honeymoon's
earliest days, had she listened so eagerly for
the music of his "footstep on the stairs"
as now she did; and when at last, he, with
the frown upon his brow which she had
learned to dread, entered the room, she flew
to him, and placed the rescued fragments
of Time, and fire-stained paper in his hands.

"Read these," she cried excitedly; "almost every word is there! Emily Vidal
has sent them to me. Here is her letter;
and oh, Wilfred, won't you believe now
that she is not wholly bad? She
felt sure that seeing the notes would
make you forgive me at last, and so
she snatched them from the fire."

With her small hands clasped tightly
on her husband's arm, Florence watches,

as she reads, the dark brow relax; and when she sees a smile creep over the stern lips which a drooping moustache does not wholly hide, she says, less timidly than before, while her brown eyes glance up into his masterful face,—

"They are not so *very* wicked, are they, dear?"

"Wicked!" he repeated, with a laugh, which, if she had not been so overwhelmingly happy, would have rather provoked his wife. "Why, you foolish little woman, I never read such childish nonsense in my life. And you actually gave six hundred pounds, or whatever it was, for this rubbish? Forgive me for laughing," he adds, as he winds his arm round his wife's slender waist, "but it really has been such a storm in a teacup, that I cannot help it."

He had watched the gathering of tears in the pleading eyes of his wife, and dreading, after the fashion of his sex, the scene which to his thinking is imminent, he has spoken in a light and jesting tone; but the kiss which he presses on the carnation-hued lips that are so near his own, speaks volumes, not only of forgiveness of the past, but of a love which Florence whispers to her happy heart will last till Death shall them part.

May's wedding-day arose bright and cloudless, and the child bride, as she stood with her "second love" before the altar, was haunted by no self-reproachful memories of her first sweetheart. Time and Nature had played well their parts, and she was happy.

Sir Wilfred responded gracefully to

the question of "Who giveth this woman to be married to this man?" and his parting good wishes to the bridegroom were, owing to his renewed belief in his own sweet wife, uttered with peculiar hopefulness and zest. He was still of opinion that young army men had better steer clear of matrimony, but *nemo mortalium omnibus horis sapit*, and if his dear friend Cranston should be so fortunate as to find in pretty May a second Florence, why Life, Sir Wilfred told himself, might yet for that best fellow in the world, possess its charms.

THE END.

COLSTON AND COMPANY, PRINTERS, EDINBURGH.

www.ingramcontent.com/pod-product-compliance
Lightning Source LLC
Chambersburg PA
CBHW020107030726
47498CB00006B/1992